"Be my girlfriend.

"We can announce it was love at first sight and let them take the story from there."

"G-girlfriend? That will make them more interested in me and Jayden. And neither one of us wants that. I think if we lay low, maybe not see each other for a bit, this will blow over. I'm not the story—you are."

"I don't think this is the right play here, Iris."

"And your objections are noted," Iris replied, "but we're not chess pieces your PR team can move across the board. I need time to think about this."

"Time is running out, Iris." He was desperate for her to see how bad this situation could get. The paparazzi could be vicious.

He had to tell her he was Jayden's father. Only then would she see his way was the only way out of this mess.

* * *

Red Carpet Redemption is the third book in The Stewart Heirs series from Yahrah St. John.

Dear Reader,

Red Carpet Redemption is the third book in The Stewart Heirs series. My inspiration came from watching the Jennifer Lopez movie *The Backup Plan*. What if the heroine used a sperm donor to get pregnant and falls in love with him years later?

That notion gets turned on its ear when the donor turns out be A-list actor and America's Sexiest Man Alive Dane Stewart. The lovable hunk has no idea he's a father or that his son Jayden is in need of a bone marrow transplant. Navigating fatherhood and falling for his son's mother, Iris Turner, was never part of the plan, but their first meeting has Dane seeing stars. I hope you enjoy this feel-good love story.

Dane's story was to be the last book, but the series felt unfinished. Expect the fourth and final book in 2020. Visit my website for more details, www.yahrahstjohn.com, or write me: yahrah@yahrahstjohn.com.

Best Wishes,

Yahrah St. John

YAHRAH ST. JOHN

RED CARPET REDEMPTION

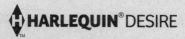

Recycling programs
for this product may
not exist in your area.

ISBN-13: 978-1-335-60406-4

Red Carpet Redemption

Copyright © 2019 by Yahrah Yisrael

Printed in U.S.A.

Yahrah St. John is the author of thirty-one books and one deliciously sinful anthology. When she's not at home crafting one of her spicy romances with compelling heroes and feisty heroines with a dash of family drama, she is gourmet cooking or traveling the globe seeking out her next adventure. St. John is a member of Romance Writers of America. Visit www.yahrahstjohn.com for more information.

Books by Yahrah St. John

Harlequin Desire

The Stewart Heirs

At the CEO's Pleasure
His Marriage Demand
Red Carpet Redemption

Harlequin Kimani Romance

Cappuccino Kisses
Taming Her Tycoon
Miami After Hours
Taming Her Billionaire
His San Diego Sweetheart

Visit the Author Profile page
at Harlequin.com for more titles.

You can also find Yahrah St. John on Facebook,
along with other Harlequin Desire authors,
at www.Facebook.com/harlequindesireauthors!

To my husband and best friend,
Freddie Blackman,
for helping keep me grounded.

Prologue

"We have to clean up your image, Dane," his publicist, Whitney Hicks, informed him while they sat in his trailer in Mexico, going over Dane's public appearances for late July. It was blazing hot and he'd come in to get out of the heat.

"It's not my fault," Dane Stewart responded, leaning back on the sofa and propping his legs on the sofa arm. "I had no idea Lia Montgomery was taken. I pride myself on having one relationship at a time and being a one-woman man."

"Who according to tabloids can't stay with one woman."

Dane shrugged his broad shoulders. "Can I help it if a woman can't manage to hold my attention?"

"You're going to have to learn," Jason Underwood

replied. Jason had been his manager and agent for years. He was tall, lean and always in a suit. "Negative publicity could damage your image as America's Sexiest Man Alive."

"I beg to differ. I think it shows what a hot commodity I am," Dane said with a smirk. He was thirty years old and in his prime.

"Thanks to your shenanigans, the studio wants you to do some damage control. They don't want this kind of publicity attached to what essentially is your best acting work. You could get a best actor nomination for your latest film. Think of how this would catapult you into the stratosphere."

It had taken Dane years of callbacks and tending bar to be in the position he was in now. He didn't have to act in the big budget action flicks or romantic comedies anymore. Instead, his success in Hollywood had finally allowed him to choose a passion project like the film he'd just wrapped. Dane was proud of the work he'd done and didn't appreciate the press making him out to be some Neanderthal who couldn't keep it in his pants.

"Although I think this is all a load of hogwash," Dane responded, "I agree now isn't the most convenient time for this to blow up. I want my work to define me, not what I do behind closed doors."

"Good. Then you'll agree to the publicity I have scheduled?" Whitney inquired.

Dane trained his eyes on her. "Depends on what it is."

"You'll like this one." Whitney reached for the remote to turn on the television and start a recording.

Dane watched as a local newscaster talked about a young boy, six-year-old Jayden Turner, who was in need of a bone marrow transplant. The camera panned to the cute boy with a mop of curly hair and dark brown eyes. The doctor talked about Jayden's acute lymphocytic leukemia in which the bone marrow made too many white blood cells. He went on to say the best form of treatment was a bone marrow transplant. Then the camera zoomed in on Jayden's mother, Iris Turner, a tall, slender woman with a beautiful smile.

Iris pleaded with the public to register to have their bone marrow screened. Dane immediately sat upright and listened to her impassioned plea. He admired her quiet strength. There was a tranquility to her he was drawn to, even though she wasn't a dazzling beauty like many of the models and actresses he usually dated.

"Let me guess. You want me to be screened?" Dane asked over the hum of the television.

Whitney beamed. "Great minds think alike." She walked toward him and he scooted aside, making room for her. "This is exactly the kind of positive press you need."

"I won't make a mockery of what that mother is going through," Dane stated vehemently.

"And we're not asking you to," Jason chimed in. "Just a photo op after the screening. Your involvement will be a huge help raising awareness for Jayden's cause."

Dane inhaled deeply, staring at the screen. The mother was staring back at him and he could see how desperate she was for a chance to save her son's life. "I'll do it."

Whitney grinned. "I'm glad that didn't take too much convincing. Now here are my other ideas."

Dane listened as Whitney rattled off several other appearances, including late-night television, a morning talk show and a stop at the local food bank, but all he could see was the haunting eyes of Iris Turner. Dane hoped his presence at the hospital wouldn't disrupt her and Jayden's life.

One

Iris Turner was praying for a miracle. She didn't know when or in what form it would come, but she knew God wouldn't be so cruel as to take away the precious gift He'd given her six years ago. Her son, Jayden.

"Do you think it will help?" her mother, Carolyn, asked as Iris sat at her parents' kitchen table, wringing her hands. It had been several days since the news story about Jayden had aired, and there was still no bone marrow match.

"I don't know. I hope so." Iris glanced down the hall to where her father and Jayden were playing in the living room. To the outside world, he looked like a normal kid; now all of Los Angeles knew how sick he was.

"It will." Her mother reached across the short distance to squeeze her hand.

Her family had thought Iris had lost her mind when she'd decided to become a single mom. Her mother had discouraged Iris, telling her Mr. Right would come along one day, but Iris had known it wasn't true. She was damaged goods and no man would want to sleep with her—let alone make a baby—if he saw her body in the dark.

Eight years ago, when she was twenty, she'd gotten mixed up with the wrong crowd, dating a musician who liked to drink and have fun. One night, he'd had a little too much fun and wrapped his car around a tree with Iris in it. She'd suffered severe burns to her arms and thighs. Iris had lost count of the reconstructive surgeries she'd had since then to help with the disfigurement. Her arms had been transformed almost back to their original state, but after many painful procedures, Iris had finally given up and accepted she wouldn't be completely healed.

She'd attempted dating, but once the evenings had become intimate, men had shuddered, making a speedy departure. Some were more direct; one outright told her she was a monster. Iris hadn't dated since.

"Let's not dwell on it." Her mother went over to the stove and removed the kettle she'd turned on earlier. "How about a cup of tea?"

"Sounds great, Mom." Iris offered a smile. Her mother was not only her best friend but an excellent cook and homemaker. She'd always been there when Iris needed a shoulder to cry on or someone to accompany her to the endless medical treatments. Iris had wanted to be just like her, and part of that was having a child of her own to love and being the best mom she could be like her mother.

Six years ago, she'd decided the only way she'd become a mother was through artificial insemination. And it had worked! She'd become pregnant on the first try. Nine months later, she'd given birth to a beautiful baby boy. Recently, she'd learned her precious boy had a rare leukemia that couldn't be treated with chemotherapy alone. The doctor had suggested that a bone marrow transplant could be Jayden's best chance.

Iris accepted the cup of tea her mother handed her and took a tentative sip. Chamomile always had a way of making her feel calm, and she was summoning all her inner strength for the fight ahead.

Her cell phone rang and she answered after several rings. "Hello?"

Iris listened intently to the caller on the other end before hanging up the line. "You will not believe it, Mom. It was the hospital. Their phones are being flooded with callers who want to know how they can help Jayden and if there's a GoFundMe page."

"I told you it was going to work out, Iris. You just have to believe."

Iris was beginning to think her mother was right. Maybe there was a miracle waiting around the corner for Jayden.

"So what's this I hear about you dating another man's girl?" his sister, Fallon, asked Dane over the phone that day.

"Not you too," Dane said, padding into his kitchen

in his bare feet. He removed a beer from the fridge, unscrewed the cap and took a generous pull.

"I've never known you to do anything so under-handed."

"Then you have to know I didn't think she was see-ing someone."

Dane loved being single and the freedom it gave him. He'd always done uncomplicated sex but now this disaster with Lia Montgomery had blown up in his face.

"All right, so what now?"

"Damage control," Dane said, drinking his beer. "I'll put in some appearances, be contrite and do some charity stops. Actually, I'm kind of excited about the one tomorrow."

"Oh really? What's it about?"

"There's this young boy who needs a bone marrow donor and I'm going to have myself tested."

"Dane! That's wonderful and very selfless."

Dane shrugged as he walked to his patio door and slid it open. The balmy ocean air wafted into the room, filling his senses. He loved his Venice Beach house, which he kept in addition to his mansion in the Hol-lywood Hills. It had cost him a mint, but the view of the Pacific out his back door was worth every penny.

"Yeah, well. I'm being tested. There's no guarantee."

"It's the thought behind it."

Dane wished he could take credit, but it was Whit-ney's doing. "So," he said, changing the subject, "when are you, Gage and that good-looking nephew of mine coming down for a visit? You haven't been here in ages." Fallon had recently married Gage Campbell, a wealthy financier who'd help save the family business and she'd given birth to a son, Dylan.

"I'm sorry, Dane. Getting Stewart Technologies back on its feet took a great deal of time. With Gage's influx of cash, I've been able to get new research in the works to put us back on the map but that's taken a while. I promise we'll come soon."

Dane never understood Fallon's devotion to their father's company and her sense of responsibility for its survival considering their parents had run it into the ground with frivolous spending. He'd offered some financial resources over a year ago when it appeared the company was on the brink of failure, but she'd turned down his offer, determined to save the company on her own.

"Good. 'Cause I miss you, sis."

"Back at you."

From his patio, Dane stared out over the darkened horizon and thought about his family. Ever since he'd been able to read, their father, Henry Stewart, had talked to Dane about taking over the company, but it hadn't been his dream, and when he was old enough he'd run as fast as he could. Fallon had taken up the mantle and Dane was glad because, quite frankly, he'd never lived up to his father's expectations. The rumors of Dane's scandalous behavior had only added fuel to the fire.

But what did he care? Dane didn't need anyone. Or at least that's what he told himself. As long as he had a winning smile and there were beautiful women around, he would never be alone for long.

The next morning, Dane arrived at Cedars-Sinai Medical Center and was immediately engulfed by a large, noisy crowd of fans, mostly women. Some were holding banners with his picture; others screamed how much they loved him and wanted to have his babies. Dane reminded himself this was all part of the price of fame.

After climbing out of the low-slung seat of his Ferrari, several bodyguards surrounded him as photographers flashed cameras and journalists shot questions at him. Dane waved and signed a couple of autographs as he strode into the hospital entrance.

Whitney came toward him. Her bouncing blond hair hung in luxurious curls down her back and she was wearing her customary dark pantsuit. Dane appreciated her professionalism.

"Come with me." She led him down a long corridor to an elevator that within seconds had them disembarking onto the pediatrics floor.

Whitney moved ahead of him, and they soon stopped in front of two glass double doors leading to a room with brightly colored walls. "It's a play area for children in the hospital. I thought it would be a good place to start, but Ms. Turner isn't here yet."

Dane glanced into the room and his heart clenched. There were several young children in the room. Two were in wheelchairs and the other three were at low tables coloring. He vowed at that moment to give a donation to the hospital; it was the least he could do.

He heard the chime of the elevator and the hairs on his neck stood up. Dane knew Jayden Turner and his mom had arrived. He turned around in time to watch Iris Turner walk toward him. She was a lot taller than she appeared on television and every bit as slender in a pencil skirt and ruffled blouse. She was much prettier in person.

There was a youthful glow to her unblemished caramel skin, big brown eyes and dark brown hair, which fell in soft waves past her shoulders. His body tightened, reacting to her beauty, and Dane tamped the feeling down. He didn't mess around with single moms—that was borrowing trouble he didn't need. But he couldn't deny he was drawn to her.

"Dane, I'd like you to meet—" Whitney began, but he interrupted her.

"You must be Iris Turner. Pleasure to meet you."

"You, as well." She offered a hesitant smile. "Thank you so much for doing this. To have someone of your stature…" Her voice trailed off as Dane's focus shifted to her son. "I'm sorry." She blushed. "This is Jayden. Jayden, say hello to Mr. Stewart. He's here to see if he can help you."

"Help me?" The little boy looked up, and Dane froze.

With his tight black curls, dark brown eyes and bushy eyebrows, Jayden bore a striking resemblance to Dane when he'd been young. Dane shook it off. He must be projecting because he felt sorry for him. He kneeled down. "I'm here to see if I'm a match to help you get better."

"Why would you do that?" Jayden asked.

The innocent question caused all the adults in the room to laugh. "Because it's the right thing to do." Dane responded.

"Do you mind if we get a few photographs?" Whitney inquired from behind them. Dane had been so engrossed with meeting Iris and her son, he hadn't noticed that a photographer had entered the room and was snapping away.

Iris glanced at Whitney and then back again at Dane.

"Only if it's okay with you," Dane said. He sensed fear in her eyes, and he didn't want to take advantage.

Iris nodded. "Yes, of course."

"You mind if I pick you up?" Dane asked Jayden.

Jayden immediately held out his arms and Dane eased him into his embrace and stood.

The photographer asked Iris and Dane to move closer together into the frame. "Yes, like that. Smile, please. Heck, if I didn't know any better I'd say you guys looked like a family."

Iris quickly glanced up at Dane, but he merely laughed.

Within minutes, the photographs were taken and the nurse led Dane away for the cheek swab test that would register him as a bone marrow donor. Due to Jayden's aggressive leukemia, they would have the results back within a week. The entire process was over with quickly, and Dane realized Iris and Jayden hadn't needed to be there. It was merely a photo op to show America Dane wasn't some lothario who couldn't be trusted, but for him it was more. It was a chance to shed light on the issue of bone marrow transplants.

When he was done, Whitney was waiting for him in the corridor. "That's it for today. For the next couple of days, you'll have a full calendar of appearances and events, which will hopefully bring up your approval ratings."

"Am I being rated?" Dane inquired.

"Well, no, but we do informal polls on your image," Whitney replied. "It's my job to ensure you have the right kind of press."

"I appreciate it. Now if you'll excuse me." Dane headed for the playroom. He could still make out Iris's form through the glass doors. He was curious to know her story.

"Where are you going?" Whitney inquired.

Dane didn't answer. "If the PR stunt is over, you can leave. I'll see you on the plane tomorrow." He spun away and went inside the playroom. He found Iris huddled over the blocks with Jayden. As he approached, he noticed a wariness come over her and it made Dane nervous. "Hey."

"Hi."

"The testing didn't take long, so—I was wondering if you wanted to grab a cup of coffee and maybe a cocoa for the little man." Dane looked at Jayden, who was oblivious to them, too caught up with building a large tower with the blocks.

"Just us?"

Dane grinned. "You mean, you don't want my entire

entourage?" He glanced behind him to find the body-guards were guarding the door. "Yes, just us."

She nodded. "Okay, sure."

Dane lent his hand and helped Iris up from the small chair. He was surprised when an electric shock surged through him at merely touching her. He was aghast at having a reaction when Iris was here with her sick child, and quickly stuck his hands in pockets.

Iris swallowed and tried not to show how hurt she was by Dane recoiling from her. When he'd touched her, she'd felt the zing low in her pelvis, awakening sensations she had almost forgotten. Her heart had fluttered, making her breath catch in her throat, but it was clear Dane was disgusted. Since he had no idea about her injuries, his reaction had to be because he found her lackluster. In comparison to his latest dalliance that she'd read about online, Lia Montgomery, Iris was sure she was. She'd perked up when he'd asked her to coffee, but now she understood it for what it was: pity.

It didn't stop her from staring at Dane from underneath her lashes. He was startlingly good-looking. With his hair cut short, his face was a marvel up close, all creamy tapioca skin, strong clean jawline, dark brown eyes, bushy ebony brows and tempting mouth. Dane was movie-star handsome and downright sexy without even trying. Take what he was wearing today, for example. The leather jacket, T-shirt and faded jeans were what any joe on the street would wear, but a woman could forget herself completely in his smile and would be thankful she had.

Impossible images flashed in her head of Dane without any clothes on. Each one was more inappropriate and more unlikely than the last. She blinked to clear her thoughts.

They made it to the cafeteria with the two bodyguards flanking them. After the two men had surveyed the place, she, Jayden and Dane were allowed to make their way to a four-seater table.

Iris was surprised when Dane pulled out her chair and scooted it underneath her before sitting across from her. When Jayden began to get fidgety in his chair, she reached inside her purse and fished out her iPhone. She handed it to him and watched with amusement as he found his favorite video game.

"Regular coffee okay?" Dane asked. "Or are you one of these LA women who drinks a soy latte with no foam or something?"

His low, rich voice washed over her like a caress and her body melted. "Nothing fancy for me," Iris said. "With Jayden's illness, I've gotten quite used to regular ole coffee from the hospital cafeteria."

"Two regular coffees coming up," Dane said, rising again to his feet. "And what about you, Jayden?"

"He'll have milk."

Jayden glanced up at Dane. "You promised cocoa."

A broad smile spread across Dane's sensuous lips. "So you do listen when you want to," Iris teased, ruffling his curls affectionately. She looked at Dane. "A cocoa it is."

"One cocoa and two coffees coming up." Dane sauntered away and Iris couldn't help but watch him. The man had swagger. Lots of it. And a great behind to boot. She couldn't believe someone as famous as he had the time to spare for her. Iris was nobody's fool. She understood part of today's exercise had been to garner good press for Dane. But if seeing a famous A-list actor like Dane registering to become a donor could help Jayden, she would take a hundred pictures with him.

Dane returned several minutes later carrying two steaming cups of coffee and a cocoa with whipped cream on top for Jayden. "How did you manage that?" Iris wondered aloud.

"I have my ways," Dane said with a smirk, his dark eyes gleaming.

Jayden immediately began drinking his cocoa and got a white mustache. "Go wipe your face, Jayden," Iris said, laughing as she watched him get up to find napkins.

"So tell me, Iris—is it all right if I call you Iris?"

"Yes."

"Where's Jayden's father?"

Iris frowned. "That's a very impertinent question to ask."

"I'm sorry. I wondered where he was in all this and why he wasn't here supporting you both. I'm sorry if I overstepped."

"No, I'm sorry," she apologized. "I suppose I'm overly sensitive. It's just me and Jayden. Though my parents have been wonderfully supportive since he was diagnosed."

"How long ago was it?"

"About three months," Iris replied. "Jayden wasn't

gaining any weight and was weak and lethargic, so I took him to the doctor. They ran a battery of tests that were initially inconclusive, but I knew something was wrong."

"A mother's intuition?"

"Something like that. I refused to give up so they kept digging and eventually Jayden was diagnosed with a form of acute lymphocytic leukemia."

"Had to be hard hearing the news. I mean, he's so young."

"Yes, it was very difficult, especially when I learned how hard it would be to find a donor. And then here you are."

"Don't make a saint of me just yet," Dane responded. "I'm only registering."

Jayden returned with the napkin and Iris used it to wipe his face, catching the spots he'd missed. "But you're doing something and that means so much to me," she said, meaning every word as she glanced up at Dane. Whether he was a match or not, or had just come to the hospital to boost his image, he was here, and it could mean the difference between life and death for her son.

"What else can I do to help Jayden?" Dane glanced down at her son with genuine concern. "I feel like getting tested seems so small in the grand scheme of things."

"It isn't. I wish more people like you would register. I think there's a stigma attached to bone marrow donations because people have seen it on TV and heard it can be painful. But they've made advances and there's more than one way to donate now."

"I'll certainly make sure to talk about registering when I make the rounds on the morning and late night shows."

Iris's eyes grew large. "You would do that?" She gulped a large amount of coffee in an effort to steady herself and not think about why Dane Stewart would help her, a nobody.

"Of course. Anything to help this little guy." He glanced down at Jayden. "He should have his whole life ahead of him and if there's anything I can do to prolong it, I will. Matter of fact…" He reached inside his leather jacket and produced a business card, handing it to Iris.

Her eyes filled with tears and instinctively she reached for Dane's hand on the table to squeeze it. "Thank you."

This time he didn't pull away. Instead, he let her hold his hand a moment longer than was necessary. Iris's heart bounced like a ball in her chest as she relived the excitement from his touch earlier. Her tummy fluttered and she could feel her breasts becoming taut as awareness flooded her entire being. She bit down on her lip, but when she glanced up at Dane, raw primal lust was etched across his face.

Dane took in the glorious brown eyes staring back at him. Sensation galloped in his chest from the shocking contact and enveloped him like wildfire. He'd felt it earlier too and it made him want to touch her shiny dark brown hair. Their gazes clashed and mingled and something unspoken fizzled in the air between them. Something Dane couldn't define. Was it lust?

He was taken by surprise because there was an answering hunger in her quiet gaze. Dane reminded himself he was repairing his public image, and to even consider messing around with Iris at a time like this would be low. Yet he couldn't stop himself feeling this pull toward her and the boy. He wanted to be there for her, comfort her, *protect* her.

With his self-discipline vanishing, Dane abruptly rose to his feet. "I have to go."

Iris did the same, and he noticed how she nearly matched him in height. "Of—of course. I'm sorry to have kept you." She blushed alluringly as if she shouldn't have been caught looking at him.

"You didn't, but I have an early morning tomorrow."

"Thank you again for registering."

Dane crouched down to say goodbye to Jayden, who'd already finished his cocoa. "I hope you get better, Jayden. I'm rooting for you."

Jayden glanced up. "Thanks, Mr. Stewart."

The young boy's smile in spite of all he'd been through broke Dane's heart, and he quickly made for the exit without looking back at Iris. He couldn't. Instead, he pulled out his cell phone, made a call and snapped out instructions.

The bodyguards followed him to the lobby and out through the main entrance, where his car had magically appeared, along with Whitney, who was now by his side barely keeping pace with him.

"What was that about?" she asked.

"What?" Dane was disconcerted. He was still thinking about the beautiful woman he'd left upstairs whom he'd given his private number to. It was something he never did, but Dane felt like he could trust her.

"Iris Turner. You asked her to coffee."

Startled, Dane glared at her. "I'm not sure what you're implying, Whitney. I was merely being nice. I would think you'd appreciate the positive press instead of twenty-questioning me." He didn't wait for a response as he hopped in his sports car.

Adrenaline, sleek and sure, pounded through him as he revved the engine. Had the truth been written on his face? Could Whitney sense his interest in Iris? Her hand was so delicate, yet strong. He could *still* feel her touch as if she'd branded him, which was ridiculous. She was going through a lot and for some reason Dane wanted to help her. And if it was in his power to assist, he would.

There was nothing more to it than that.

Two

One week later

"You're a match," Dr. Lee said.

It was early on a Monday morning, and she and Dane were seated in the conference room at Cedars-Sinai. Dane had flown in last night from New York after the premiere of his latest film. It was a departure from his usual body of work and would finally elevate him from heartthrob to serious actor. Early reviews were positive and Dane had left on cloud nine.

He hadn't expected this news.

"Really?" Dane asked, stunned. He'd registered and done the test when he'd been trying to repair his bad boy image. It had worked. The press began to focus on Jayden's illness and the media lost interest in his supposed affair with Lia. He'd been so busy doing damage control, he hadn't contacted Iris. It was just as well because he couldn't act on his attraction to the single mother.

This was an unexpected wrinkle in his plans. "How is that possible? I thought chances were rare I would be a match." He stared in disbelief.

"It's difficult to match the needed tissue type between donors and patients, so this is quite a surprise. Seventy percent of all bone marrow donations do come from people unrelated to the recipient, so only 30 percent come from matches with family members able to donate. And when I compared your genetic markers to Jayden's, there was no doubt—you're related."

Dane sat back in his chair. "Pardon me?"

"If I was a betting man…" Dr. Lee began, then paused for several beats. "I would say that you're Jayden's father."

"No," Dane shook his head and jumped to his feet. "That can't be. I never met Iris before last month. You've got this all wrong, Dr. Lee. There's no way Jayden could be my kid. You need to run your tests again." His mind raced to recall a moment he could have met Iris. A drunken encounter he could have forgotten maybe? But no—that wasn't possible.

Dr. Lee sighed. "Well, that's why I wanted to bring you in. Quietly, of course." He looked out the glass partition at Dane's two bodyguards waiting outside. "I wanted your permission to run a DNA paternity test."

Dane stopped pacing. "A DNA test?"

"Yes, it will give us irrefutable evidence and set the record straight."

"That depends. Do I have your word you'll treat this with absolute discretion? I can't have this leaking to the press."

"Understood. And you absolutely have my word I'll keep this confidential. But in the meantime, I need to know if you're willing to donate your bone marrow to Jayden. Whether you're his father or not, you're a match. I'd like to take a sample of your blood and confirm the human leukocyte antigen match. Once I confirm, you'd meet with a counselor to talk about the procedures, benefits and risks of the donation process. And then you can decide whether you're comfortable with donating."

Dane wiped his hands across his face. This was surreal, but he was sure of one thing. "Of course I'll help. That was never the question. Jayden is a very sick little boy and from what I've heard he doesn't have much time. But I need to know if he's my son."

Dr. Lee rose from his seat. "Excellent, Mr. Stewart. Ms. Turner will be so relieved but probably shocked once she hears of the connection."

"She can't know," Dane replied.

Dr. Lee frowned. "What do you mean? I need her permission to run a DNA test."

"I understand that, but," Dane pronounced, "under no circumstances am I going to rip that family to shreds and have the press crawling through their lives if this is merely a case of mistaken identity. This has to be kept under wraps until we can run a test."

"I understand you're apprehension about the DNA test, but it's more of a formality for legal purposes. I'm certain the additional blood test you're required to undergo will further confirm you're Jayden's father," Dr. Lee replied.

"I don't know. Let me figure this out. What I need from you is discretion. Promise me, Dr. Lee, you will keep this between us until we know more."

"All right. I'll keep your genetic connection to myself, but I'd like to give her some hope and at least tell her you're a match. Let's reconfirm the match."

Dane nodded his acquiescence. "I'm here, so let's do this."

Two hours later, Dane slid into the back seat of the SUV waiting for him outside a secluded section of the hospital. For once he was grateful to be alone with his thoughts, so he could absorb the bombshell Dr. Lee had dropped on him. Dane had reacted on autopilot throughout the testing, not caring one bit about being poked and prodded. Now that he was done, he was finally free to feel, well, dumbstruck.

Jayden Turner could be his son!

But how? He'd never met Iris until that day a month ago. And since then he'd pushed all thoughts of the slender beauty out of his mind. Until now. One thing was certain: if they'd ever met, Dane was sure he'd *remember* her.

Then it came to him.

Eight years ago, he'd arrived in Los Angeles to make a fresh start. Considering he'd snubbed working for his father, Dane had been determined to live on his own without any help from his family. However, he'd quickly learned how expensive it was to live in the city and after toiling at two, sometimes three jobs he'd barely made ends meet. A year in, he'd had a particularly rough patch, when he'd blown off work to go on some auditions. Dane knew he'd be discovered. He hadn't been. Instead, he'd found himself without a job. Desperate to pay the rent, he'd taken the advice of several other starving artists and gone to donate at a sperm clinic. They'd happily accepted him since he fit certain criteria and he'd signed a contract for a few months. He'd never thought it would come to anything, but he had been selected once. And apparently once was all it took.

It was highly possible Iris had used his donation. Jayden could very well be his.

Dane felt like he couldn't breathe. He didn't need Jason or Whitney to tell him the fallout over this decision could be massive. They'd finally gained momentum for the movie and now…now he had a son? And a son who was fighting for his life, no less. Dane didn't even know how to comprehend the barrage of emotions hitting him. Iris had been handling Jayden's illness all alone for months. Heck, she'd been a mother and father to Jayden. If Dane was truly the father, how would she react to his sudden appearance in their lives?

It was all too much to contemplate. He was so lost in thought that he was stunned when the SUV came to a stop in front of his Hollywood Hills home and his bodyguard Doug opened the door for him. He was already home.

"Thanks, Doug." He nodded at the three-hundred-pound former college linebacker as he strode inside. He was hoping for some time alone, but instead found his assistant, Morgan, along with Whitney and Jason, lounging around on the couch in the living area.

Morgan was a twenty-four-year-old film school dropout who'd been working for him for over a year. They'd met on the set of one of his films, and she'd begged him to give her a job, any job. At first, Dane had been reluctant. Five feet six with long, silky black hair and hazel eyes, Morgan could have been trouble. But Morgan had never looked at him as anything other than a big brother and typically dressed in gender-neutral clothing. She was a godsend and kept his life on track.

"There you are," Jason said from his perch. "We were starting to think we were going to have come get you. How'd it go?"

"I need the room," Dane said, directing a look at Morgan and Whitney, who took the hint and made a speedy exit. He headed for the bar and quickly produced two glasses and a bottle of aged brandy. He poured generously and pushed a glass toward Jason, who'd come to join him at the bar. Even though Jason was his business manager and agent, Dane considered him a friend. For years, Dane had been able to rely on Jason's advice and he prayed he wouldn't fail him now.

"What's going on?" Jason asked, sitting across from

Dane who'd remained standing behind the bar. "What did the hospital say?"

Dane stared at the brandy in his hand for a moment and then took a large gulp. It burned on the way down.

"Easy now, Dane. Whatever it is, spit it out and we'll deal with it." Jason reached for his brandy and sipped.

"Jayden Turner could be my kid."

Jason spluttered as brown liquid spilled from his lips. "What did you say?"

"He could be mine. Jayden could be my son."

"That's impossible." Jason quickly snatched a napkin from the countertop and wiped up around him. "If there's one thing I know about you, Dane, it's that you practice safe sex. Whatever this Iris is saying about you is a lie. I don't know if she sensed your interest in her or what, but it's fabricated. Don't worry. We'll fix this."

"You don't get it, Jason. There's nothing to fix," Dane responded. "I donated sperm seven years ago and Jayden is probably the result."

"You did what!"

Dane rolled his eyes. "Don't look at me like that. I was low on cash and rent was coming due. It was a high-end clinic with a very selective process. I was only selected one time."

"One time that could be Jayden?" Jason inquired.

"Ding-ding-ding! You're finally getting it. And I have no idea what to do."

"We need to confirm it," Jason stated, "so we can get ahead of the story before the truth gets out. Spin it."

"Jason, if he's mine, there's no spinning. I will claim

him," Dane responded. "I'll do what's right. And if he's not, I'll still donate."

"This is big, Dane. Are you sure you're ready for the heat this could bring? Not just for your career, but personally? To my knowledge, you've never wanted to be a father."

Jason was right. Dane didn't see himself like his brother and sister, settling down and having a family. He'd always been the odd bird and that had been fine with him. His career had always been his central focus, but now he could unwittingly have a ready-made family waiting in the wings.

Iris was on cloud nine.

Earlier today, Dr. Lee had called and informed her there was a match for Jayden. For months, she'd thought it was a pipe dream. She'd gone on television and begged people to register to donate, but she'd never actually thought anything would come of it.

"Are you sure?" she'd asked him, and she'd given her an unequivocal, resounding yes. But nothing could have prepared her for her next words when she'd asked who the match was. It was none other than Dane Stewart, the man who haunted her dreams day and night.

Since their meeting, Iris had found herself searching out his movies and watching them, either on television or Netflix. She'd become obsessed with seeing him on screen, with his sexy good looks and killer abs. Maybe it was to remind herself how strictly off-limits a man like Dane was. And she'd done a good job. She'd convinced herself she'd imagined the connection between them in the cafeteria because Dane had better options than a harried single mother.

Iris had just put Jayden to bed, and was finally ready to retire for the evening. But as she went into her bedroom, she decided there was one more thing she needed to do. Reaching for her purse, she pulled out the business card Dane had given her. Iris had never thought she'd have the opportunity to use it, but she felt compelled to thank him. Dr. Lee had told her donating was much easier these days and that they could do a peripheral blood stem cell donation, but it was still a procedure that might have some recovery time. Dane was a working actor, so it meant a lot that he was willing to make the personal sacrifice for Jayden's benefit.

Without thinking, she grabbed her iPhone and dialed his digits. *He's not going to pick up*, she told herself, *he's not going to pick up*. But he did.

"Hello," a deep masculine voice said from the other end of the phone.

"Dane?"

"Yeah?"

"Hi, um, it's…it's Iris Turner. Jayden's mother," she began. "I hope it's okay I called. You gave me your cell at the hospital—"

"Iris," he interrupted her, "relax. It's fine. You're not bothering me. I was hoping you'd call."

"Really?"

"I assume you heard the good news. I'm a match for Jayden."

"Yes." She breathed a sigh of relief. He wasn't upset

she'd phoned. "Dane, I'm so thankful you're willing to donate."

"Of course I'll donate. Jayden has his whole life ahead of him. I want the best for him."

"You do?"

"Yes. I'll clear my schedule whenever I'm needed."

"Thank you. Will you let me know when the procedure is? I'd like to come if that's all right with you."

"Absolutely. It's going to be okay, Iris. Jayden will pull through this. We'll see to that," Dane said.

"You make it sound like we're in this together."

"We are. I now have a vested interest in Jayden's recovery."

"Is that all?" The moment the words were out of her mouth, Iris wanted to take them back, but she couldn't. They lingered, floating on the air.

There was silence for several beats, and Iris was wondering if she'd overstepped when Dane said, "No, it's not all, Iris. I've thought of you often since our meeting."

"You have?" Nervous excitement raced through her veins. Had her initial intuition been right? Dane was interested in her?

Dane chuckled. "Don't sound so surprised. You're a beautiful woman, Iris. I'm sure you know that."

"It's been a while. We single moms don't get very many compliments, especially not from America's Sexiest Man Alive."

"Aw, don't believe the hype, Iris. I'm a man like everyone else."

"Yeah, but you always have a beautiful woman on your arm."

"Those are hookups," Dane admitted. "I don't date. Not really. Because I don't know if they're after my money or if they really want me, you know?"

"That's terrible, Dane. How do you live with it?"

"Not very well. I'm the actor everyone wants in their movie, but sometimes the whole machine of my reputation and brand swallows up the real me. Yet when I talk to you, all the chatter melts away and I feel like myself."

"I'm glad, but what about your family? Aren't they there for you?"

"No, not really. They have their lives and I have mine, but I do check in with them from time to time."

"I don't know what I would do without my family," Iris replied. "They keep me grounded."

"Then you're lucky indeed," Dane said. "Hold on a minute, Iris. What's that?" Iris heard voices and realized he was talking to someone in the room with him, but couldn't make out the conversation. When he returned, he said, "I have to go, Iris, but I'm glad I have your number now. I'll save it in my phone. I'll be seeing you soon."

"All right. And Dane?"

"Yes?"

"Thank you. You're a lifesaver."

Dane sucked in a deep breath as he ended the call with Iris. Morgan had called him on the intercom and he'd used it as an excuse to get off the phone. Leaning back in the executive chair in his study, Dane stared at the ceiling. He hadn't anticipated hearing her sweet voice again so soon, but he supposed he shouldn't be surprised. Iris wanted to thank him for agreeing to donate his stem cells. What she didn't know was that Jayden could be Dane's son too.

All that was left was the additional blood work and a DNA paternity test, but Dane didn't need that. He'd felt an instant connection to Jayden from the start.

But it was six years too late, in his opinion. He had a son who needed bone marrow. And *his* would save Jayden. Fate, the cosmos or something was sending him a message. He hadn't figured out what it was yet.

All he knew was that if he was going to be a father, he didn't want to be like Henry Stewart. But was he being premature? Would he even be able to carve out a parenthood agreement with Iris? It was entirely possible she would fight him on any visitation arrangement, given that he was just a sperm donor.

But perhaps the even bigger question was…how would this affect his career?

Three

Fallon, it's Dane. I really need to see you. I'm flying into Austin tomorrow. In the throes of a full-blown panic attack, he'd called her in the wee hours.

Now, as Dane boarded the private jet he'd anonymously booked to fly him to his hometown that morning, he thought back on recent events. He knew the voice mail he'd left for his older sister was cryptic, but he needed to talk to someone who knew him. Who understood him. Who would listen without judging. Iris was right. He needed his family. Fallon had always been his sounding board, so here he was, on his way to Austin.

The flight was smooth. After renting a nondescript SUV, Dane drove through the city toward Fallon and his brother-in-law Gage Campbell's home, which wasn't far from Stewart Manor. No matter what, he couldn't keep his mind from spinning.

Deep in his gut, Dane knew he should tell Iris the likelihood that they shared a son, but quite honestly, he was afraid of her reaction. What if she refused to let him see Jayden? She might think he'd set all this in motion as a way to get closer to his son when that was far from the truth. He'd had no idea of Jayden's existence until a two weeks ago, but that might not stop her from thinking the worst. He was already a scoundrel for the feelings he had for her.

When she'd called him last night, they'd shared such an easy rapport. Dane hadn't been able to talk to someone like he was just a normal guy in ages. Maybe it was the novelty factor. Iris wasn't the kind of woman he usually dealt with. She wasn't trying to flatter him or cozy up to him because she wanted a role in his next film. She just wanted to talk to him and it made Dane feel like everyone else, which had been sorely lacking in his world. Was that her appeal?

When he arrived at the Campbell residence, he punched in the security code and the black wrought-iron gates opened. There was a long driveway leading up to a château-style mansion with a well-manicured lawn and tall topiaries. Immediately upon exiting the vehicle, the front door opened and his sister came running out and into his arms.

"It's so good to see you, Dane," Fallon said softly.

He was in his usual casual attire of faded jeans, T-shirt and worn leather jacket. The jacket had seen better days, but it was the one item of clothing he'd bought with what he'd earned from his first paid acting gig and he'd kept it ever since. "You too, sis." He squeezed her back. Eventually, he pulled away and gave her the once-over.

Fallon was still an absolute stunner in her cape top and slender trousers. She wore her honey-blond hair in its natural curly state rather than straight the way she usually did for her job as CEO of Stewart Technologies.

"You're looking good, girl. How's Dylan?"

Fallon beamed, which caused her hazel eyes to sparkle. "He's doing fantastic. C'mon inside and see for yourself." She slid her arm through Dane's and walked him inside.

"I'm surprised you're home. I would have thought you'd be out conquering the tech world instead of playing happy homemaker."

Once in the foyer, Fallon came to a halt. "First off, I will never be a homemaker," she responded. "I have a great staff here to help. Plus, I doubt Gage would let me. He and Dylan demand all my attention."

Dane laughed. "So married life is going well? I know you and Gage got off to a rocky start."

His sister hadn't married Gage for love. It had been a marriage of convenience to help save Stewart Technologies. Dane and their older brother, Ayden, had offered to pitch in monetarily, but Fallon hadn't accepted. She'd chosen to marry Gage in exchange for his funding instead.

Dane had worried about the union, but he supposed he shouldn't have. He and Fallon had grown up with Gage while Ayden had lived apart with his mother who raised him. Ever since her teens, Fallon had had a huge crush on Gage and had never really gotten over him. It turned out the feeling had been mutual, so what had started as a temporary arrangement ended up becoming a real marriage.

"That's all in our rearview," Fallon replied. "I hope one day you can find what Gage and I have, not to mention Ayden and Maya."

"How is that older brother of ours?" Dane inquired.

"He's right here," Ayden bellowed from several feet away.

Dane spun around and was surprised to see his older brother, casually dressed in jeans and a pullover sweater, holding Dylan. "What are you doing here?" The question came out harsher than he'd intended.

"Well, since you barely ever come home, I had to get in where I can fit in," Ayden replied, bouncing the eleven-month-old baby in his arms. "I'd like to get to know you better, Dane, but you don't make that easy."

Dane shrugged. "I'm sorry. Life's been…challenging."

"Care to fill us in?" Fallon asked, folding her arms across her chest.

"Sis, that's exactly why I'm here."

A half hour later, Dane had had brought Ayden and Fallon up to speed on the details, including his hard times that had led to his donation to a sperm bank. He confessed his sample had been used once and Jayden Turner was most likely the result. Fallon was so bowled over, she called the nanny to come get Dylan so they could discuss the matter in private without interruption.

"Wow!" Ayden scrubbed his jaw and leaned back in his chair. "Are you certain he's yours?"

Dane nodded. "When I registered to become a bone marrow donor, I took some tests. When the results came in, Dr. Lee was surprised Jayden and I shared genetic markers. She asked me to come in privately to talk about it. Initially, when she suggested I could be Jayden's father, I thought she'd lost her mind, but upon reflection I recalled the sperm donation. So it makes sense that Dr. Lee's hypothesis is true."

"Have you taken a DNA test? Are you ready to be a father and all that it implies?"

"Hell no!" he said, jumping to his feet. "I'm not ready for any of it. But I'll know more soon after the additional blood test results come through."

"The press is going to have a field day with this." Ayden had just spoken Dane's worst thoughts aloud.

"I know, I can handle them ripping me to shreds. I'm used to it. But Jayden and Iris? They don't deserve what's in store. Jason and I have been figuring out a way to protect them."

"You told your *agent* before you told us?"

Dane heard the censure in Fallon's question. "I did. And I'm sorry, but I'm here now. Don't I get credit for that? Do you have any idea of the media storm that's about to rain down on me?"

Fallon stood and walked over to him, grabbing his hand. "I do. And you know Ayden—" she glanced at their big brother "—and I will be here for you. We can't wait to meet Jayden and his mother."

"Iris."

"You're on a first-name basis with her?" Ayden inquired.

"Yeah, we've talked a couple of times and I met her when I registered to become a donor. She is an amazing woman. Beautiful, strong and a dedicated mother."

Ayden's brow rose. "Is that right?"

Dane hated that his brother could tell he wasn't being completely forthright. "What's it to you?"

"Nothing, Dane." Ayden shrugged. "But I suspect there's more to you and Iris than you're telling us."

Fallon's gaze clashed with Dane's. "Are you two involved? Because if you are, it will only compound the problem. Being attached to you carries a huge spotlight."

"Well, thanks a lot, Fallon. And for your information, we are not involved," he responded.

"Not yet," Ayden offered. "But if you can't be honest with your family, who can you be honest with? You came here because you needed to unload. Do that. I know I'm not as close as you and Fallon, so if you need me to leave, I will."

Dane glared at him. Ayden was right, but that didn't make it easier to hear. "All right, I'm sort of interested in Iris. I gave her my private number and we spoke the other night, but I haven't acted on my attraction to her."

"But you want to?" Fallon deduced.

"Yeah, but I know it's not good for either one of us. I'm keeping my distance, but when she learned I was a match for Jayden, she offered to come to my procedure for emotional support."

"And you agreed?" Ayden asked.

Dane nodded. Why were his siblings ganging up on him? "Is that so horrible?"

"Of course not, but you could have called either of us," Fallon glanced in Ayden's direction. "We'd hop a flight and be there in a heartbeat. The truth of the matter is, you didn't want us. You want *Iris* to be there."

Fallon had hit the nail on the head. "You may be right," Dane finally admitted. "But I can't let her do that without telling her the truth."

"But you're afraid of how she may react?" Fallon asked.

"Can you blame me?" Dane asked. "This whole situation is bizarre. I want to do what's right and help save my son…"

"But you also want his mother," Ayden surmised. "I'm not sure it will be quite so easy to have your cake and eat it too, Dane. Iris is going to be extremely conflicted. On the one hand, you're saving her son's life, but on the other, you bring an entire media firestorm."

"Which is why I've been trying to figure out how to insulate her and Jayden from the fallout."

"Is that really possible, Dane?" Fallon said. "I mean, you might be expecting too much."

"I'd expect to hear that from the pessimist over here—" Dane motioned to Ayden "—but not you. You're supposed to be the optimistic one."

"I am, but I'm also a realist," Fallon responded. "I've had to be."

Dane knew what Fallon meant because they'd always understood each other so well. She'd been levelheaded about business, a pragmatist who'd saved

Stewart Technologies. But she also blamed herself for letting their father's mismanagement and their mother's spending habits wreak havoc on the family company. "It wasn't your fault, Fallon."

Ayden peered back and forth between the two of them. "What wasn't her fault?"

"She thinks she let Father ruin the company."

"You didn't *let* him do anything," Ayden responded hotly. Dane smiled because it didn't take much for his brother to pick up the torch. There wasn't any love lost between Ayden and their father. "Henry is responsible for his actions. And Nora too."

"I know you are not a fan of our parents." She glanced at Dane and then at Ayden. "And justifiably so considering how our father treated you, so let's agree to disagree on this, okay? Dane…" She turned to him. "You need to tell Iris. If you wait too long, she'll resent you for keeping this from her. Tell her. And tell her soon."

He stayed with his siblings for the remainder of the afternoon. He didn't intend to stay long. Dr. Lee was rushing the blood test and Dane wanted to be back in LA in case he learned Jayden was indeed his. Fallon suggested visiting their parents, but Dane was in no mood for Henry to gripe about him throwing his life away to be an actor. Instead, he met up with his old friend Jared Robinson for a beer. Jared came from a wealthy family and was a rabble-rouser like Dane had been back in the day. They reminisced about old times when chasing women was their number one hobby, but those days might soon be behind him.

* * *

The next morning, Dane hadn't forgotten Fallon's advice to tell Iris and he intended to tell her Dr. Lee's suspicion when he landed. His plans, however, didn't fall into place like he wished. When he'd arrived home, Morgan filled him in on his new schedule and he'd been annoyed. Instead of time to meet with Iris, Dane found himself the following day at a photo shoot in downtown Los Angeles warehouse.

"Don't be mad," Whitney said as a stylist trimmed Dane's perpetual five o'clock shadow early that afternoon. "We have to take advantage of every opportunity to plug your movie. You want a blockbuster, right?"

Dane stared at her crystal-blue eyes in the mirror. "I wouldn't make it a habit of going against my wishes, especially when I give you a directive to clear my schedule."

"Of course, I'll get with Morgan and make sure your schedule is clear for the next couple of days."

"Thank you."

Dane was desperate to talk to Iris about Jayden. *His son.* The words still sounded foreign. Probably because he hadn't gone through the normal process like most people where you had nine months to prepare for becoming a parent. Dane was being thrown in the deep end of the ocean without a life jacket. On the jet ride home last night, he'd downloaded several books on parenthood and was reading them voraciously. He understood he had a lot of catching up to do.

Jayden might even be angry at him for not being there and Dane would have to accept that, even though it would hurt. When he'd signed up to be a sperm donor, he hadn't thought about the consequences. If he could go back, Dane was certain he'd make a different choice, but he couldn't regret he had a son. Someone with his genes. His DNA coursing through his veins. He would do anything to help him, even putting aside promotion of his new movie, which had been his baby from the moment he'd signed on to play the role. Because Jayden's health now took precedence over everything else.

When the photographer signaled he was ready, Dane walked over to the set. He was in the same attire he usually wore, except this time the jeans and T-shirt were supplied by the stylists. He went through the motions, striking the requisite poses.

When Dane finished an hour later, Morgan was waiting for him with her tablet in hand. "I have the car to take you to the beach house."

Dane smiled. Morgan was a saint. She knew exactly what Dane needed after a long day trip to Austin. "Thanks, Morgan. I'll check in with you later." He waved at the photographer, thanked the stylists and left.

Within minutes, he slid inside the Bentley waiting for him outside in the alley. Thankfully, security had surrounded the warehouse, preventing the press from getting in. Several paparazzi shouted his name as he did, but Dane was weary and quickly closed the door. Within seconds the vehicle took off blessedly toward home.

They arrived at his Venice Beach house nearly an hour later because of traffic. After punching in the code, Dane closed the door and sagged against it. He was dog-tired. Plopping down, he drifted asleep. It was nearly 5:00 p.m. when the ringing of his cell phone woke him up. "Hello?" he said without looking at the caller ID.

"I'm sorry. You sound like you were taking a nap. I must have woken you up. I'll call back later."

Instantly, Dane bolted upright. "Iris?"

"Yes."

"Is everything okay? How's Jayden?" Dane was surprised how quick he was to think about the boy.

"I'm fine. He's fine. It's just… I—"

"You what?" He could tell she was hesitating.

"I made a rather large pan of baked ziti and… I don't know, it's silly, but I thought you might like to join us for dinner if you weren't too busy."

Dane felt the broad grin spreading across his face. "It's not silly at all. I can't remember the last time I was invited for a home-cooked meal. I would love to come, but it'll take a minute to talk to my security detail so they can help me lose the paparazzi. I'll take my bike, but I'll be there within the hour."

She let out what sounded like a sigh of relief. Did she think he would turn her down? "Okay, great. We'll see you then. I'll text you my address."

Dane stared down at his phone. He was actually going to get to spend time with his son. This was beyond great, but it was also an excellent segue for him to talk to Iris. He hoped he could find the words.

Four

Iris smoothed down the one-piece V-necked jump-suit she'd changed into. It was casual enough to wear around the house on a Wednesday evening, but was nice enough to entertain in. She didn't want Dane to think she was trying too hard.

She'd been surprised when he'd accepted her invitation to dinner. Since their talk, she hadn't been able to forget him. Despite his fame and obvious good looks, he was approachable and she'd found the connection between them wasn't one-sided. Dane could have said no, he was too busy, but instead, he was coming to her humble abode.

The roar of the motorcycle engine brought Iris over to the window in time to catch Dane swinging one muscled leg over the bike and onto the sidewalk. Iris's heart thumped loudly in her chest. Dane Stewart was about to walk over the threshold of her house. It was almost too much to process. *Almost.* Instead, she took a deep fortifying breath and opened the door. Dane stood on the other side, looking hot and holding up flowers and a bottle of wine.

"Can I come in?"

"Of course." She motioned him inside and blatantly stared at him. "It's kind of surreal having you in my living room."

"I couldn't turn down a home-cooked meal from a beautiful woman."

"Dane…" She blushed. He was a charmer.

"You're nervous," Dane observed, taking off his leather jacket and throwing it over the arm of her sofa. "Don't be. I *wanted* to come." He handed her the flowers, an assortment of peonies. "I brought these for you." He placed the bottle of wine on the cocktail table.

"Thank you." And she was nervous. It had been years since she'd been on a date, much less had a man in her home. It was nice to feel young and carefree and revel in the fact she was with a gorgeous man like Dane. "I'll put these in water."

She made for the kitchen and once there, leaned against the sink trying to regain her composure. "Get it together, Iris." She placed the flowers in a vase and brought them into the dining room. On her way, she grabbed two wineglasses from her cupboard and the corkscrew from the drawer.

She found Dane standing by the fireplace, looking intently at the pictures on the mantel. There were various photos of Jayden and a family portrait of the Turner clan. There were none of Iris before her accident; she couldn't bear to see how she *used* to look because she would never look like that again.

"Would you like to open the wine?" Iris inquired and noticed he jumped as if she'd caught him doing something he shouldn't.

"Uh, yeah, I can do that." Dane accepted the corkscrew and set about opening the bottle. "Where is the little fella? I was hoping to spend some time with him." Dane sat on the sofa while Iris chose the adjacent love seat.

"For now, it's just me," Iris responded. "I hope that's okay? Jayden's at tae kwon do. I wanted him to have an activity that develops good character. They teach self-esteem, courage, courtesy, self-respect, focus and discipline. If you knew what it was like wrangling a six-year-old, you'd understand. Anyway, he should be here soon. My neighbor's son also takes tae kwon do, so we rotate picking them up from class each week. It allows me to get dinner started so Jayden isn't eating too late."

"That's great. I'm glad you have a support system. I'd hate to think of you doing this all alone." When he released the cork, he poured them each a glass and handed her one.

"Thank you, but I'm not alone. My parents, my sister, Shelly, my neighbor—they're all part of the village it takes to raise Jayden. Cheers." She tapped her wineglass against his.

The front door of the bungalow sprang open and Jayden bounced excitedly into the room.

"Mommy, you should have seen me tonight!" Jayden rushed over to her, not even noticing Dane on the sofa. He was still wearing the standard white *dobok* uniform consisting of a top, elastic-waistband pants and a belt. "I did a better ax kick than TJ."

Iris smiled broadly. "That's great, Jayden. Say hello to Mr. Dane. You remember him, right?"

Jayden spun around and hazarded a glance at Dane. "Yeah. You're the man who is going to be my donor." And without her asking, Jayden threw his arms around Dane's neck. "Thank you."

Tears sprang to Iris's eyes as Dane held Jayden in his arms. He seemed as overcome as she was by Jayden's spontaneous affection. "You—you're welcome, Jayden." Dane patted his back and just that quickly, Jayden was moving on.

"I'm hungry. What's for dinner?"

Iris rose to her feet and picked up his book bag, which he'd left in the middle of the floor. "Your favorite—baked ziti and garlic bread. Go wash up. Dinner will be ready shortly." Jayden scampered out of the room, leaving the two of them alone again.

"Sorry about that. Jayden can be a bit extra if you're not used to him."

"Extra?" Dane appeared distracted, then shook his head. "No, he's fine. Is he always that affectionate?"

"I guess. Why?"

"No reason. He's a really special little boy."

Iris grinned. "I think so. C'mon, grab your wine."

* * *

Dane followed Iris down a small corridor into a farmhouse-style kitchen with a table big enough for four, but with place settings for three. He sat down in one of the chairs and watched Iris. She busied herself taking garlic toast from the freezer and putting it in the oven.

Dane couldn't recall when he'd witnessed anything so domestic except when Gage's mother, Grace, had lived at Stewart Manor and worked as their cook. She hadn't minded him and Fallon being underfoot. Lord knows his mother, Nora, wouldn't be caught dead cooking; that would require putting in effort. The only thing Nora was good at was keeping herself well preserved with Botox and frequent trips to the gym and salon.

Iris spun around and faced him. "Is something wrong?"

"No. Why?"

"You're frowning," Iris answered. "I'm sorry dinner's not ready. I know your time is very valuable. The garlic bread will be ready in five minutes."

Dane gave a mirthless laugh. "It's not you, Iris. I was thinking about how my mom never cooked for us. She's never been all that interested in me or my sister."

"Really? What mother doesn't care about her kids?"

"The kind of mother who stole our father from his first wife and made sure to get pregnant so he wouldn't leave her."

"Surely she isn't as bad as you say?"

"Worse, but I don't want to talk about my mother." He sipped his wine.

"What do you want to talk about?"

Her question was innocuous. She had no idea of the undercurrents about to sweep her away. Dane figured the conversation could wait until after dinner. So he used his charm and changed the subject. "How about how good you look in that…" Dane tried to think of the word for the contraption she was wearing. All he knew was the difficulty in getting a woman out of one. *But not impossible.*

"Jumpsuit?" Iris offered, glancing down at her outfit. "This is really nothing."

"I don't think so." He ran his gaze over her body and the attraction he felt sizzled. She was aware of it too—that subtle shift in the atmosphere. He noticed how her nipples suddenly thrust against the fabric.

Dane stood and walked over to her, forcing Iris backward against the sink. Lifting his hand, he ran the tips of his fingers experimentally over her hair. He felt Iris tremble at the action. "Your hair feels like silk."

Iris looked up at him, and Dane felt an overwhelming urge to kiss her. He told himself to resist. He hadn't come clean with her about his discovery he was Jayden's father. Until he did, it wouldn't be right. But Jesus, he was sorely tempted. "I want to kiss you so bad." He didn't realize the words were out of his mouth until they hung in the air.

"Then why don't you?"

"Mom—" Jayden's voice startled them, forcing them to quickly step away from each other "—is dinner ready?"

"Yes. I think it is," Iris said.

* * *

After dinner, Iris didn't recall how the baked ziti and garlic bread tasted. She'd been too caught up in the illicit feelings Dane had evoked when he'd backed her up against the sink and stroked her hair. It had felt so good. It had been so long since she'd felt desire. It was as if he'd drugged her with his words and she wanted more.

Someone, however, had taken Dane's attention away from her. Who would have thought it would be her six-year-old son? The two of them were like peanut butter and jelly. They meshed. Iris was surprised at how easily Dane conversed with Jayden and vice versa. They had a natural ease around each other. Dane was very inquisitive about Jayden's likes and dislikes. Iris loved that Dane was taking such an active interest in her son, because they were a package deal.

Iris suspected he was probably bored with the women in his circle and wanted to branch out. As a single mother, Iris knew she couldn't go too far down this rabbit hole with Dane, but it was sure nice to feel wanted.

Eventually, Jayden went to bed, but only after Dane agreed to read him a bedtime story. Iris tried to talk him out of it, but Dane insisted he was fine. And so, Iris had watched from the doorway as Dane sat by Jayden's bedside in his Spider-Man–inspired room and read him a bedtime story about a prince with fire-breathing dragons until eventually Jayden's eyes closed. Dane softly crept out of the room, meeting her in the corridor.

She glanced up at him. "Dane, you really didn't have to—"

Iris didn't get another word out. His arms came around her and her chest collided with his. And any past doubts she may have had about herself ebbed away when he pressed against her. He was hot and hard, and deliciously male. He wanted *her*. That much was obvious. She glanced straight up into those dark brown eyes of his and lost the battle.

Everything exploded at the first touch of his mouth on hers. Dane took control of the kiss and one of his hands wrapped itself in her hair, so he could angle her head for a better fit. And then he simply...*took*. He kissed her deeply and Iris loved every minute of it. She shivered against him uncontrollably as a rich, heady desire stole through her body.

The passion between them was so strong, it obliterated everything else, making Iris forget they were in the hall outside her son's bedroom. So when Dane shifted to haul her against the wall, Iris didn't care; the only thing she could do was kiss him back like she was a starving woman and he was her only sustenance.

Nothing existed but the two of them in this moment as their lips and tongues tangoed in a sensual rhythm as old as time. She circled her arms around his wide, powerful shoulders, curved with muscles honed by what she was sure were many hours in the gym. When he leaned in harder, pressing his hips against hers, it forced her small breasts into closer contact with the hard wall of his chest, and Iris moaned. Heat gathered low in her belly, making her feel hot, hungry and ready—

Jesus, she was losing her mind. She hadn't behaved this way in a long time, since…since the accident. Thinking about that and what might come next was like having a bucket of cold water poured over her and Iris slowly stopped engaging in the moment.

Sensing the change, Dane pulled back. His breathing was ragged and heavy. "I'm sorry. I shouldn't have done that."

Iris lowered her eyes and shook her head. "It's not you. It's me."

Dane snorted. "If ever there was a line from a movie…"

Glancing up, Iris offered a small smile. "I don't know what came over me." She moved away from him and started toward the living room.

"Would it help if I said I didn't expect it either?" Dane said. "I didn't come over to seduce you, Iris. I genuinely care about you and Jayden."

"I can see that."

His brows furrowed. "Can you?"

"The way you were with him tonight was amazing," Iris said, turning around to face him. "Makes me realize he's missing not having a father in his life."

Here was his opportunity to come clean. To tell Iris he could be Jayden's father. By some stroke of fate, life had led them to this moment where he would be able to save his son's life, the son he never knew he had.

But Iris was still speaking and he didn't want to interrupt her. He followed her to the sofa where she'd made herself comfortable and sat down beside her. He was going to try to keep his hands to himself, but after that explosive kiss in the hall, it was going to be difficult.

"I've tried to be both mother and father to Jayden," Iris said, "but it's hard sometimes, ya know? Was tonight his way of telling me he needs more male companionship in his life? As his grandpa, my dad does his best to pitch in, but I wonder if I made a mistake."

"A mistake?"

"I don't know who Jayden's father is because I had Jayden through artificial insemination." When Dane remained quiet at her revelation, Iris asked, "You don't want to know why?"

"Only if you want to share." He had wondered. Iris was a beautiful woman. What would make her decide to take such a drastic action? But he couldn't ask that. He had no right to judge her, considering he'd been a sperm donor himself.

Iris shrugged. "I… I wanted to be a mother," she admitted. "And I wasn't sure it was going to happen for me. My family was dead set against it. They tried to talk me out of it, but I was determined. And wouldn't you know, I got pregnant on the first try! What are the odds? Anyway, that's the long and short of it. I thought I understood how hard it was going to be, being a single mother." She glanced down the hall. "But I guess I was wrong."

He had to say something. This was the perfect opportunity. He wasn't going to get another one, but where did he start? "Iris, I—"

"Mommy, I'm thirsty." Jayden appeared in the living room in his Spider-Man pajamas, looking sleepy eyed.

Iris was immediately on her feet. "I'll be there in a minute, honey. Go on back to bed."

Rubbing his eyes, Jayden didn't argue and went to his room.

"It's going to take me a minute to put him back to bed." Iris glanced down at Dane. "I should walk you out."

No. This couldn't be happening. She was asking him to leave now, when he was on the cusp of telling her he was Jayden's father? "Iris, we should really talk," he began.

She nodded. "I know, but it's late and I should get Jayden back to bed. Can I take a rain check?"

Dane couldn't push his luck. The conversation they needed to have was too important to be rushed. "Of course." He grabbed his leather jacket off the sofa arm and followed her toward the door. "Thank you for having me over tonight. I can't remember when I've had such a great time."

Iris laughed aloud, and the sound was melodious. "No need to lay the charm on so thick, Dane. I highly doubt baked pasta with a single mom and her six-year-old is a barrel of fun. Not with the movie premieres, travel and stars you get to meet."

"You'd be surprised, Iris Turner. You'd be surprised." The glow of being a movie star had worn off a long time ago. Luckily, he still enjoyed the craft of acting.

Iris walked him to the door and when he got to the threshold, Dane leaned in and brushed his lips tenderly across hers. "Don't sell yourself short, Iris. Tonight was amazing." Then he was running down the stairs toward his motorcycle. He turned and caught Iris in the door watching him. He could feel her blush all the way from where he stood and she immediately closed the door. Dane remained outside for several moments, staring at the house. Inside was his son and the mother of his child, a woman who was quickly becoming so much more.

Five

Dane wished time would slow down for once and allow him to catch his breath. Since his dinner with Iris a week ago, he felt as if someone had pressed the gas pedal to the floor. Dr. Lee had rushed the results as anticipated. Now Dane knew with 100 percent certainty that Jayden was his. He was both excited and overwhelmed. Rather than tell his family and friends, Dane was taking time to digest the news.

One thing was taking longer than he'd expected, though. He'd thought that the procedure for Jayden would be in a few weeks, but once he went to the information session about acute lymphocytic leukemia, he'd quickly realized his error. It would be at least a month before Jayden was ready to accept his bone marrow. Dr. Lee explained Jayden would have to have daily chemo treatments before his immune system was wiped out. Only then would he be able to receive Dane's healthy stem cells.

Meanwhile his team ran full steam ahead with his normal slew of activities. When he wasn't promoting his new film, he was reading scripts for his next project and working through callbacks for his next leading lady. He wasn't excited about another big blockbuster, but the only way Jason had gotten the film studio to agree to his passion project was if he agreed to do a sequel to a megahit he'd done two years earlier.

Competition was stiff for his new leading lady but so far the readings were ho-hum in his opinion. Dane supposed that was why his mind was always drifting to Iris and that one incredible evening they'd shared.

Iris haunted him.

Her taste. The sounds she'd made when she'd moaned out her enjoyment during the heated kiss in the hall. The sweet scent of her fragrant perfume. He found it impossible to concentrate on running through the scene with the myriad women the casting director brought in. Instead, Dane went through the motions. Apparently it hadn't gone unnoticed because one day Jason pulled him outside the warehouse during a break.

"Are you all right?" Jason inquired. "You're a little distracted."

"I have a lot on my mind."

"Well, snap out of it. The studio head is here and he might forget you're the star if you don't show them who's boss." He stared at Dane for several moments and then asked, "Is this about Iris Turner?"

Dane grabbed Jason's arm and pulled him farther away from the warehouse entrance. "Keep your voice down."

"Are you still hung up on this kid thing?" Jason asked. "You know, you don't have to *do* anything. You can donate your bone marrow and she can continue raising him without you ever telling a soul he's yours."

Dane stared back at him incredulously. "Do you honestly think I can go my entire life knowing I have a kid," he whispered, "and do nothing? Is that really the sort of man you think I am?"

"I'm giving you an out, Dane. In case you were looking for one. I've known you a long time and I'd hate for this situation to derail your hard work."

"And your cash cow?" Dane replied. He was Jason's biggest client and that was fine, so long as they were honest about his intentions.

"This is not about the money, Dane, and I resent you saying so," Jason responded. "I care about you. You're like my kid brother. I'm looking out for you and maybe telling you something you're afraid to think, much less say out loud. But if you need me to be the fall guy, then fine, so be it."

Dane sucked in a deep breath. "I'm sorry, Jason. This whole situation has me on edge. I should have told Iris when we had dinner."

"When did you have dinner? Did you sleep with her?"

"No!"

"But you came close," Jason surmised.

"We kissed after she'd invited me to share a meal with her and Jayden. Can you blame me for wanting to get to know my son?" His voice was low, nearly a growl. He didn't want anyone hearing their conversation.

"Of course not, but you have to be careful, Dane. You're not an average guy who can have dinner with a woman you're interested in. You're Dane Stewart."

Dane nodded. "I realize that. But she still has to know."

"Ultimately it's your decision, but in the meantime, I need you to get your head into this reading."

Dane followed him inside, but Iris and Jayden were not far from his mind. He had to figure out a way to ease into releasing the bombshell and pray Iris didn't explode when she found out.

Iris wanted to cry. Over the last couple of months she'd watched Jayden go through physical exams, blood tests and a monthly bone marrow test. But today was the worst, when the nurses put a PICC—a peripherally inserted central catheter—in his arm. It was a thin, soft tube inserted into a peripheral vein in his upper arm. It would facilitate the pretreatment for the transplant and allow prolonged and safer access to Jayden's veins to draw blood and administer chemo.

The line would stay in his arm the entire treatment. It was hard to hide and needed to stay bandaged to prevent infection, but the team at Cedars-Sinai was so great. They were making it fun for Jayden. They'd given him a Spider-Man sleeve cover to put over the bandage. Most kids would probably screech at the top of their lungs at seeing a needle, but Jayden had taken this and the battery of tests he'd been subjected to the last several months like a pro.

After the procedure was complete and they'd just gotten to the car, Iris had a suggestion. "How about some Moose Tracks ice cream?"

"I can have some before dinner?" Jayden asked.

"You absolutely can!" Iris said with a smile.

She'd buckled Jayden into his seat and closed the rear door when she felt a presence behind her. She spun around and found Dane there. "Dane! You nearly scared me to death." She swatted him with her purse.

Dane held up his hands in defense. "I'm sorry. Guess my lame attempt at surprising you wasn't the right move."

Iris placed her hand over her racing heart. "I appreciate you coming, but you could have warned me. What are you doing here?"

"Well, I was bombing at a reading for my next movie and I hadn't seen you in a couple of weeks so I figured I'd see how you both were doing. I remembered you mentioned Jayden's visit, so I took an Uber over." He glanced in the back seat and waved at Jayden, who responded with an enthusiastic flap of the hand.

"We just finished getting his PICC line in. Jayden was a real trooper."

"But it was hard seeing it." Dane said what she couldn't.

Tears welled in her eyes and she nodded.

"Come here." Dane pulled her toward him and wrapped her in his arms. Iris allowed herself to accept his embrace. There was something about the comfort she received from Dane that was unlike anyone else's. He made her feel special. So special it scared her and made her worry this thing between them couldn't possibly be real. For God's sake, he was a superstar.

Was she imagining he cared for her because she wanted it to be true? She breathed deeply, inhaling his heady masculine scent. Eventually, she tried to push him away, but he held on tightly.

"Don't treat me like a stranger, Iris," he murmured. His eyes were blazing with some emotion she couldn't read. When he cupped her face and kissed her, she wound her arms around his neck and his lips crushed her mouth. He invaded her senses, tasting her and teasing her with his tongue. Iris was so deep in the kiss she barely registered a knocking on the window. It was Jayden and he was staring right at them.

Iris blushed, stepping away from Dane. "I have to go. I mean, we're going for ice cream."

"Can I join you?"

One of Iris's brows rose. "Do you want to? I mean, you could be recognized and there would be a mob."

"It's why I brought this." Dane produced a baseball cap from his back pocket. "No one expects me to walk into Baskin-Robbins. I can hide in plain sight."

"All right, if you're game, then so am I."

"Good, because I wasn't taking no for an answer anyway." Without waiting for an invitation from her, Dane hopped in her Camry and they were soon taking off down the road.

On the way to the ice cream shop, Dane realized he was in way over his head. The more time he spent with Iris, the more he couldn't keep his hands off her.

Since their dinner, they'd talked on the phone a few times. Sometimes the conversations were long, sometimes short, because Iris would be exhausted from working all day and taking care of Jayden. And every time they spoke, Dane told himself he would tell Iris the truth about Jayden, but he pulled back. If he didn't tell her soon, it would be too late. She would be so upset by his deception she might not ever forgive him or allow him to see Jayden. And she had every right as his sole guardian.

Last week after Dr. Lee called him with the blood test results, he'd gone to see a custody attorney, who made it quite clear he didn't have any rights as a sperm donor. But given Dane's name and stature, the attorney thought it might be interesting if Dane did take her to court because it would set a precedent. Dane didn't want that. Iris was a great mother, yet he wanted a place, a small one, in Jayden's life. And he was certain with his help, Iris and Jayden could have a better life.

"We're here," Iris announced, pulling into a space across the street from the ice cream shop.

Dane immediately put on his baseball cap and turned around to Jayden. "You ready for some ice cream?"

"Yes," Jayden said.

Dane came around to the rear door and helped Jayden out of the booster seat. He saw Iris glance over at him, surprised by his behavior, but he'd done what a parent was supposed to do. And when Jayden grabbed both his and Iris's hands to walk across the street, Dane beamed with pleasure.

Despite the mild evening, there weren't many people inside. Jayden rushed toward the displays.

"Thank you for coming," Iris said.

"Who doesn't love Rocky Road?" Dane said with a smile.

When the cashier came over, they placed their orders: Moose Tracks for Jayden followed by a Jamoca Almond Fudge for Iris and a four-scoop banana split for Dane. While the cashier took care of their order, they found a booth. Iris and Jayden sat on one side and Dane on the other. His trainer would kill him for cheating on his strict high-protein diet. It was worth it, however, when Jayden's eyes lit up at his banana split.

"Want some?" Dane inquired. "Dig in."

Jayden sank his spoon into the gooey chocolate mixture and let out a sigh of pleasure. "It tastes better than my Moose Tracks."

"Have some more," Dane encouraged.

"Dane, he has his own ice cream," Iris admonished.

"I know, but there's plenty for everyone. Why don't you dig in too?" Dane said with a smirk. He doubted Iris could resist the sinfulness of the banana split.

And she didn't. Minutes later, she was plunging her spoon in and licking it off. Dane's libido stirred to life watching her tongue lick and flick the spoon. He wondered what it would be like if she used it on him in places aching for her mouth.

Iris glanced up at him, and Dane had to mask his desire.

"So does kissing make you and Mommy boyfriend and girlfriend?" Jayden inquired as he took alternating spoonfuls of his ice cream and Dane's banana split.

The unexpected yet innocent question caught Dane off guard and he looked to Iris. When she shrugged, he said, "It means we like each other an awful lot. Does that help?"

"Doesn't kissing make babies?" Jayden asked. "My friend TJ said when he caught his parents kissing, a baby popped out of his mom's belly nine months later."

Dane couldn't resist letting out a loud, rambunctious laugh. "Jayden, has anyone ever told you how funny you are?"

A wide grin came across the boy's face. "Nope. But you just did."

Dane continued laughing while making eyes at Iris and eating his split.

Eventually it got late. To go along with the strategy of hiding in plain sight, he called a Lyft to take him home.

"Are you sure? I could drive you," Iris offered.

"No, it's fine. I don't want the paparazzi to get used to seeing your vehicle. So it's best if you keep a low profile."

"All right."

When they were done, Dane slid a twenty into the tip jar and walked them to their car. Once he'd settled Jayden into his booster seat, he gave him a fist bump. "You were a big boy today. Keep it up. And if you need me, your mother has my number."

"Okay," Jayden said.

Shutting the door, Dane turned to Iris. That was when he noticed the Lyft driver pulling up outside the store. "That's my ride."

"It was fun. Thank you for coming, Dane." Iris glanced behind her. "But I don't want you to make promises you can't keep."

He frowned. "What do you mean?"

"You're Dane Stewart," Iris replied, "and you're going to be pulled in a million different directions. I don't want Jayden's hopes getting high that you're going to be permanently in his life."

"Because I'm transient, passing through, is that it?" Dane asked. The Lyft driver honked his horn. "Be right there," he yelled over Iris's shoulder. "Listen, I get it. I know this thing—" he motioned between the two of them "—came as a surprise, but I'd like to be a part of Jayden's life if only for the simple fact I'm giving him my bone marrow and I want to see him live."

Iris blushed. "Dane, I'm sorry. It's just… I I don't know—"

Dane bent forward and kissed her to silence her fears. It was a sweet, soft kiss and didn't last long because the driver was honking again, letting him know he was getting impatient. He lifted his head and said, "Stop thinking so much, Iris, and just go with the flow."

He waved, ran across the street and hopped inside the waiting car.

"Ready to go?" the driver inquired, but Dane couldn't answer because Iris was still standing there. It made him want to leap out of the vehicle and take her back home where he could make love to her until the sun rose, but instead he gave the driver his address. "Yes. Take me home."

Six

"Wake up, Romeo," Jason yelled into Dane's ears on Tuesday morning. "We've got some damage control to do."

Dane rolled over on his bed in his master suite and glanced at the clock. It read 7:00 a.m. "You know I'm a night owl and don't like getting up until at least nine."

"Well, today is not your day because you couldn't keep your hands—oh, wait, excuse me, your *lips* off a certain single mother. It's now front-page news."

Dane bolted upright, letting the covers slide away. "What did you say?"

Jason leaned forward and placed a local tabloid in his face. A picture of him in the baseball cap kissing Iris at the ice cream shop was sprawled across the front page.

"What the hell?"

"Didn't I ask you to give her a wide berth?" Jason responded. "But no, Dane's going to do what Dane wants to do."

"Don't berate him." Whitney strolled into his bedroom even though Dane was bare chested and wearing pajama bottoms. She handed him the mug of coffee in her hands. "Thought you might need this."

"I could use one myself," Jason stated cheekily.

"Not a chance, Underwood. Get your own," Whitney responded, sitting on the edge of the bed as if Dane had invited her there. "Dane and I need to have a chat."

Jason rolled his eyes. "Fine. I'll get my own coffee." He left the room.

Dane rubbed the sleep from his eyes. "Where's Morgan?"

"Morgan is downstairs," Whitney replied.

Dane threw back the covers and rose from the bed. "I'm not in the mood, Whitney." He walked to his en suite bathroom and began brushing his teeth. His publicist didn't accept his boundaries and came to watch him from the doorway.

"You broke the internet, Dane. The tabloids put two and two together and realized Iris was the mother from the photo you took at the hospital after your donor registration. Did you give any thought to the consequences of your actions?"

Dane spit out the toothpaste and wiped his mouth with a nearby towel. Then he rose to his full six-foot-three height. "Don't think you're going to school me, Whitney, like I'm some naughty little boy. I can hire you and I can fire you." He strode from the bathroom and opened the door of his oversize walk-in closet. He searched the rows of clothing, which were color-coded and in order of length, until he found some sweats. When Whitney made as if she was going to join him, he gave her an evil eye and she remained outside.

"Might I remind you," Whitney said from the doorway, "you hired me to extricate you from one media disaster and here you go creating yet another. Are you a masochist?"

Dane didn't respond until he came out of his dressing room fully clothed. Jason had returned with a mug of coffee. He seemed equally floored by Whitney's audacity.

"Whitney, you should remember *Dane* is the client," Jason said.

"I do remember," Whitney nearly growled. "I just need *you*—" she glared at Dane "—to help me help you."

"Who's the actor here? Being melodramatic?" Dane inquired, raising a brow. At his lighthearted response, Jason let out a guffaw and even Whitney smirked.

"Jesus, Dane. What am I going to do with you?" Whitney asked.

"Protect my son," Dane said fervently. He glanced in Jason's direction. They'd kept the news of Jayden's existence from Whitney, but now it was time to fill her in.

"Your son!" Whitney exclaimed. "Since when?"

"It's a long story," Dane began, but Whitney shook her head.

"Oh, no, you don't." She wagged her finger. "You

don't get to dismiss this out of hand. I need the entire story so I know how bad this is going to get."

Fifteen minutes later, Whitney sat in silence. "Did you hear me?" Dane inquired. He'd shared his sperm donation story and that Jayden was his son.

"Okay. So now you've got to give me some time to absorb the news. I can figure out how to control the fallout."

Dane resented the fact they had to do damage control because he had a child.

"He's your son," Whitney said. "We can't change that, but we show what you're willing to do for your son. Maybe do some interviews about how much you can't wait to be a father. If we can get Iris on board, maybe even have the three of you on camera." At Dane's glare, she doubled down on her argument. "C'mon, from the looks of it, you two are getting along swell if that lip-lock is anything to go by."

"Present them as one happy family?" Jason added, sipping his coffee. "I don't know, Whitney. We've always sold Dane as the sexiest man alive every woman or man wants to bed. And now he's suddenly father of the year? I don't buy it."

"I need to speak with Iris first. Tell her the truth before this blows up in her face," Dane interjected.

"No, absolutely not." Whitney shook her head. "Once she knows and tells her family and friends, the story goes viral. We need to have a narrative in place before then."

"I don't like it," Dane said. "It's dishonest."

"It's protecting your brand," she responded. "Plus

you've kept the secret this long, so what's another few days?"

She was right, but Dane hated continuing to keep this secret from Iris. She deserved to know what was going on before her life change irrevocably. Because once the press caught wind of their true connection, all bets were off. "All right, let's talk this through again…" Though Dane doubted it was possible to sort it all out. They were between a rock and a hard place, and there was no easy way to tell a six-year-old you'd been MIA from his life because you'd never wanted to be part of it to begin with.

"You've been holding out on me," Shelly said when she stopped by Iris's bungalow later that evening. It looked like she'd come directly from work because she was in a business suit.

Iris frowned. "What are you talking about?"

"Don't you play innocent," her sister responded. "I was on the treadmill when a picture of you kissing Dane Stewart popped on the screen. Apparently TMZ is trying to figure out how the single mother with a dying child caught Hollywood's hottest actor."

"What?" Iris rushed to the cocktail table and grabbed the remote. She flicked the television on and found an entertainment channel. And there it was in bright Technicolor: apparently she was Dane Stewart's latest squeeze. "Omigod!" Iris placed her hand over her mouth. "This can't be happening. He thought he was being so careful."

"So it's true?" Shelly said, forgoing the couch and

sitting directly on the cocktail table. "You're seeing Dane?"

"No," Iris denied. "It's nothing like that. We just..."

"You just fell into his arms?" Shelly offered. "I'm not buying it."

Iris twisted her hands in her lap. The flirtation and kisses with Dane were supposed to be harmless. Something just between the two of them. It had been so long since anyone had shown interest in her. Dane didn't even have any idea about her injuries because it hadn't gotten that far between them. *Yet.*

Had she allowed the kiss to get out of control when he'd been at her home for dinner, Dane might have discovered the horrible truth. She shouldn't have allowed her attraction to Dane to interfere with Jayden's care. Dane could walk away at any time. No, she couldn't let that happen. Whatever this was between them couldn't go any further. "All right, I'll admit Dane and I have been friendly."

Shelly glanced at the entertainment channel, which seemed to be running the picture of their kiss on a continuous loop. "I beg to differ."

"We've been talking on the phone and he showed up yesterday to Jayden's appointment for the PICC insertion."

"How'd that go?"

"Jayden's a trooper, but all this—" Iris motioned to the television "—is more than I'm ready to deal with."

"I'm sorry to tell you, Iris, but you should have thought about that earlier. You can't date someone of Dane's stature without repercussions."

"Date?" Iris's voice rose. "It wasn't a date, for Christ's sake. He took us out for ice cream."

"And then he kissed you for the entire world to see." Iris huffed.

"Listen, sweetie." Shelly reached for her hand. "I'm not saying you shouldn't grab every bit of happiness you can find. I know Jayden's illness has taken a toll on you, but you also have to be realistic. Any involvement you have with the man could threaten Jayden's transplant. Think about it, sis—Dane is a superstar and the media is interested in his every move. And if you're with him, your every move."

"I didn't sign up for this."

Shelly shrugged. "But here we are. You need to talk to him right now. Come up with a plan of attack."

Iris pulled her hand away and jumped up. "When do I have time to do that? I'm busy taking care of Jayden, making sure everything is all wrapped up at school so he can finish out the next few weeks before we have to homeschool him." She sighed and took a deep breath. "I'm sorry, Shelly. I don't mean to jump on you. I'm overwhelmed."

"That's why I'm here. To help out any way I can."

Shelly was right. She needed to call Dane because her and Jayden's anonymity were about to be obliterated.

Iris didn't have to wait long. Shortly after Shelly's visit, her cell phone rang. The display read Dane.

"Iris, I'm so glad I reached you." Iris loved hearing his deep, masculine voice. "How are you? How's Jayden?"

"We're fine," she replied. "For now."

"So, you know we've been discovered?"

"Yes."

"I'm sorry, Iris. I should never have…" His voice trailed off.

"Should never have what?" Iris was curious what he was about to say. Was he regretting spending time with her? "Whatever it is, Dane, just tell me."

"I should never have gone to the ice cream shop without my security properly vetting the place. Someone must have recognized me and alerted the press."

Iris breathed a sigh of relief. She'd anticipated Dane saying he wished he hadn't gotten involved with her. She knew it was naive to hope someone like Dane would stay interested in her for the long haul, but it had been nice the last fortnight having someone to talk to, sharing her fears and concerns.

"I wish I could tell you I knew how to handle this," Iris responded, "but this is way out of my wheelhouse."

Dane chuckled. And she was glad he could laugh and didn't blame her for any bad publicity. Or was that an oxymoron? Was publicity bad? Lately notoriety was as equally sought after as praise. "Of course I wouldn't expect you to know how to deal with this," Dane said. "It's why I hire people."

"And do they have any suggestions?"

"They do, but I'm not sure you're going to like them."

"That sounds ominous."

"Didn't intend it to be," Dane replied. "But if I'm putting all my cards on the table, you should know I had a bout of negative publicity. I turned it around over the last month after the hospital photo shoot with you and Jayden, but the paparazzi are still out for my blood. They're going to try to put a negative spin on this."

"Why would they do that? You're donating your bone marrow to Jayden and helping save his life. That's a good thing and somehow that message is being lost."

"The tabloids are always looking to spin the story and make it seem tawdry. Make it more about us."

"How can they? We're just friends," Iris said.

"Is that all we are, Iris?" Dane said softly.

Suddenly, her throat felt dry and constricted and she knew somehow she wasn't going to like what came next.

"If I'm honest," Dane said, "I think we're *more*. But *more* in my world comes with a lot of challenges. The media will want to know everything about you and Jayden. They'll be relentless in researching you. They may even try to find dirt to make what's between us feel sordid, but I don't want that to happen. Call me selfish, but you've been a breath of fresh air and I don't want to lose you."

"Did anyone ever tell you you come on strong? We've only known each other a short time and I'm expected to answer you now?"

"Yes. I have to know where you stand, so I can protect you and Jayden. Even if we don't continue, there will be some heat if the media thinks there's some teeth to the story."

"So I'm in this either way?" Verbalizing it was scary, but she appreciated Dane's honesty. She had to state her answer.

Dane was nervous. He didn't know what Iris was going to say. He knew Whitney felt presenting a happy family for the press was the best play, but Dane didn't want Jayden or Iris to be subjected to their scrutiny this early on. He had to shield them for as long as he could. "Iris?"

"I've enjoyed our nightly phone chats."

"So have I. You have no idea how hard it is to find someone who's genuine in my world. I find you fascinating."

"Dane…" Her soft sigh came through the phone.

"I know it seems crazy I'm asking if you're in this with me when we've barely gotten to know each other, but that's the only way I can protect you. Protect Jayden."

"I'm his mother. I should be protecting Jayden."

Dane wanted to spit out the truth that he was Jayden's father. It was his job to protect him too, but instead he went with the status quo. "Of course you are, but I can help. I have a lot of resources at my disposal that can help make your and Jayden's life more comfortable. Please let me."

"Exactly what are you asking me?"

This conversation wasn't going exactly how he'd envisioned. He'd assumed Iris would go along, not be a protective mama bear looking after her cub. "Be my girlfriend. We can announce we're seeing each other.

Tell them that after meeting at the hospital, it was love at first sight and let them take the story from there."

"G-girlfriend? That will make them more interested in me and Jayden. And neither one of us wants that. I think if we lay low, maybe not see each other for a bit, this will blow over. I'm not the story—you are."

"I don't think this is the right play here, Iris."

"And your objections are noted," Iris replied, "but this is my and Jayden's life you're talking about. We're not chess pieces your PR team can move across the board. I need time to think about this."

"Time is running out, Iris." He was desperate for her to see how bad this situation could get. The paparazzi could be vicious.

"I have to go, Dane. We'll talk soon." Iris ended the call before Dane could get another word in edgewise. It was the first time one of their chats ended so abruptly and he was perturbed. He paced the terrazzo floors of his balcony and wondered how he was going to get Iris to listen to reason. At the end of the day, Dane realized, he didn't have a choice. He had to tell her *he* was Jayden's father. Only then would she see his way was the only way out of this mess.

Seven

Iris was on edge. She had been since last week when she'd spoken to Dane. She'd thought giving herself some breathing room would make it easier but it hadn't. And Dane had been persistent. He'd left voice mails and texts for her to call him. He wanted to see her, but Iris wasn't ready. She wasn't ready for any of it.

Every morning when she'd dropped Jayden off at school or left to go to work or the grocery store, she'd waited for a reporter to jump out of the bushes and ask about her relationship with Dane. But it hadn't happened. She and Jayden had been able to go on with their daily lives. They'd regularly gone to Dr. Lee's office and Jayden had started his pretreatments for the transplant.

Dane's stem cells were an incredible gift. But was

she grateful enough to act like his girlfriend? Not that she would have to do much acting—she liked Dane. But she was scared of the world he lived in. She wouldn't want to subject Jayden to it when he was fighting for his life. And what were Dane's expectations anyway? Would he expect intimacy from her? Because no matter how much she might want to, she would die inside if she had to see a look of disgust or pity in Dane's eyes if he ever saw her scars. She'd have to say no.

But everything changed this morning when she and Jayden left the bungalow only to be surrounded by members of the press. She saw the news truck parked at the curb. Reporters yelled at her and bulbs flashed brightly in her eyes.

"Iris, how long have you been seeing Dane?"

"How long have you been lovers?"

She wanted to wring their necks. How dare they yell such things around a six-year-old boy? Iris shielded Jayden as best she could by pulling him closer and whispering for him to lower his head.

"Please let me pass," she yelled, but they wouldn't stop. It was the last question tossed her way as she was settling Jayden in the back seat that got her attention.

"How long have you known he was your sperm donor?"

Somehow Iris closed the rear door, but she was sure the media got what they were looking for in her stunned reaction. She sat in the driver seat and didn't start the engine. Her mind was swirling with their questions. Could it really be true that Dane Stewart was the sperm donor she'd used for her artificial insemination? No. She shook her head. It couldn't be true. She went to a reputable clinic whose donors were anonymous. Dane couldn't be Jayden's father, could he? If he was, it would explain why Dane was such a great match for Jayden—*they shared genes*.

If this was real and not all just a dream, the question was, did Dane know? Was his interest in her some elaborate cover-up to conceal the truth that he was Jayden's biological father?

It was too early in the morning to drink, but it was Friday somewhere so Dane went out to his living room and poured a stiff one at the bar. He had to. His worst fear had materialized when he'd rolled over in bed and reached for his iPhone. News of him being Jayden's father was on every major social media and news site. *Damn*. He'd turned on the television and several channels were showing footage of Iris leaving her home and being besieged by the press. He wished she'd agreed to his protection days ago when he'd offered it. The reporters had barely given her room to enter her car. But what Dane couldn't forget was the stunned expression on her face when one of the reporters rudely yelled out asking how long she'd known Dane was her sperm donor.

Dane sipped his brandy and waited. Iris had called. Her voice had been clipped, strained when she asked if he was home. He knew why and had given her the address to his place in the Hollywood Hills. She'd told him to expect her within the hour, and Dane wasn't looking forward to the conversation. He drank more because he felt guilty. He could have prevented this, if he'd been honest with her as soon as he'd found out. Instead, he'd waited and they were paying the price.

The doorbell rang and Dane bolted upright on the sofa. Slowly, he placed the tumbler down on the table and stood. With leaden feet, he walked toward the door. The moment of reckoning was here.

He just wasn't prepared for what greeted him.

A slap.

"How dare you, Dane Stewart!" Iris strode past him into his home. After calling in sick to work, it had taken Iris nearly an hour to get to his house. She'd steadily had to dodge reporters who'd been in pursuit of her from the moment she'd left her bungalow. They'd followed her to Jayden's school, where she'd had a serious talk with the principal, informing the rather flustered woman under no circumstances should anyone be allowed to speak to or take Jayden off campus without her express consent. She needed to get her mind around what was happening, but the more she drove, the less Iris felt in control of her life.

Dane was Jayden's father. She was fairly certain of it. How else to explain his sudden interest in her in the weeks after the photo op? He'd known the only way to get close to Jayden was through her. She not only felt diminished but angry she'd allowed herself to be used. Why hadn't she seen the signs? An A-list Hollywood superstar wouldn't look twice at her. Yet she'd fallen for his charms hook, line and sinker. She felt like an idiot. And she'd come here to tell him what she thought of his deception.

Eventually, she spun around to find Dane had followed her into what could be described as a room worthy of an Italian palazzo. It was enormous, with high ceilings, marble floors and furniture that must have cost a fortune. Iris tried not to act like a country bumpkin with her mouth hanging open. Instead, she glared at him.

Surprisingly, Dane showed remorse and lowered his head.

"Do you have anything to say?"

He glanced in her direction, "What would you like me to say, Iris? That I'm sorry all this happened and you and Jayden were pulled into the circus? Then hear me—I'm sorry."

"Are you sorry for lying to me?" she queried, folding her arms across her chest.

His brow furrowed. "What do you mean?"

"Really, Dane. Are you honestly going to play dumb? How long have you known? How long have you known Jayden was your son?"

He didn't answer. Instead, he walked past her, barefoot, in the same loose-fitting jeans and T-shirt he liked to sport, and reached for his tumbler on the table. She watched him take a sip and nearly asked for one herself. She was so tense she was about to explode, but she needed to keep her head on straight. "Well? I'm waiting for an answer. And I'm not leaving here until I get one."

Slowly, Dane turned to face her. "I've known there's

a possibility for a while. After I registered, Dr. Lee called me in a week later and told me I was a match. I was happy, Iris. I could help a little boy. But then she hit me with the news Jayden and I shared certain genetic markers that were too close to be coincidental. He told me it was likely I was Jayden's father. A follow-up blood test all but proved it."

"Dr. Lee knew and didn't tell me?"

"I implored her to keep it confidential until we could take a paternity test."

"And exactly when did you think that was going to happen? Were you going to go behind my back to obtain some of Jayden's hair or saliva?"

Dane snorted. "Nothing so melodramatic. I was going to ask you and tell you the truth that there was a chance Jayden was my son. I tried calling you the last couple of days, but you ignored my calls and my texts."

"Are you blaming me for the mess we're in? You had plenty of time to tell me but you chose not to. Why did you let me believe you liked me, wanted something m-more?" Iris's voice cracked and she moved so he couldn't see her face.

She felt Dane's hands on her shoulders moments later as he turned her around. "I never lied to you, Iris." He looked into her eyes and Iris had to remind herself not to read too much into it. But her body betrayed her; she felt the sudden thrust of her nipples against the silk of her button-down shirt. "Not about us." One of his large hands reached out and his fingers drifted through the strands of her brown hair.

How was it that one touch from him made her senses

jangle? The familiar desire she always felt around Dane was making her breathless in a way she didn't want to be. Iris pushed her hands against his chest to get some breathing room. "Yeah, yeah, yeah. You found me fascinating. The plain Jane who needed a sperm donor so she could get pregnant. How you must have laughed about me to your team."

"Stop it, Iris. Stop putting yourself down. I won't have it."

Iris laughed. As if he could stop her from the downward spiral she'd felt since the moment she'd woken up in the hospital after the car accident to find out she'd been disfigured, most likely permanently.

Dane clearly didn't understand the change in her. "Why are you laughing?"

"Because. This situation is so contrived. It's like something out of a bad Lifetime movie of the week." She did her best impersonation of a voice-over. "'Famous actor falls for single mother with dying son.' Except this time the joke is on me because the actor in question also happens to be his father."

"Iris, I had no idea of Jayden's existence. If nothing else, believe that."

"Oh, I believe it," Iris said. "I doubt someone like you purposely wanted to make a baby."

He winced at her harsh words. "That's not fair, Iris. You don't know the situation. It's not fair to judge me."

"Well, then, enlighten me." She moved over to a chaise and plopped down. She eyed him as he walked to the couch adjacent to her and sat down.

"I was a starving actor. Low on cash. A friend of

mine told me a clinic was looking for the cream of the crop to use as sperm donors. He said with my looks, I would be a shoo-in. Of course it wasn't as easy as it looked. There were lots of exams, blood work, questionnaires and the like, but eventually the clinic used me. And I just forgot about it because I was discovered and my career was blowing up. I vaguely recall getting a letter once about being selected, but it didn't register until after I left Dr. Lee's office. That's when I realized Jayden could be mine."

Iris sucked in a deep breath. "Thank you for the backstory. It helps me see exactly where we stand."

"And where is that?"

"You said it yourself—you never wanted to be a father. You never gave a thought to the possibility of a child."

Dane's face turned red, and she could see she'd struck a nerve. "And so in your opinion, I'm disqualified from being Jayden's father? Who are you to judge me, Iris Turner? You're the one who went to a sperm clinic and got artificially inseminated."

"Because I wanted to be a mother," Iris railed, "and all that entailed. *I* have been in Jayden's world from the moment of conception. *I* carried him in my womb for nine months." She pressed her hand to her stomach. "*I* gave birth. *I*'ve raised him the last six years."

"I know that," Dane responded, "and I'm not discounting any of it. You're an amazing woman, Iris. I've said so from day one. But I know Jayden exists now. He's real to me. And he needs me. He needs his father."

"Does he? Because up until now he has done quite

fine without one," Iris responded. But she knew she was lying to herself; she'd seen how different Jayden was when Dane was around.

"I disagree."

"Does it matter now? You've brought down hellfire on all of us because you're in his life, in my life. I don't even know what to do next."

"I would like to take the paternity test."

"No."

"Iris, you're being unreasonable. You may want to deny this is happening, but the truth is already out there. Kids are going to talk. We need to explain to Jayden what's going on."

"*We* don't have to do a darn thing," Iris replied. "*I'll* talk to him."

"When?"

"Don't press me, Dane. Jayden is my child."

"And he's probably mine too. You can't cut me out."

"After all your lies and deception, I can do what I please. You could have just told me the truth and left me out of this entire debacle, but you had to come in and play hero like in one of your movies."

Dane stared back at her for several long moments before saying, "What's got you more upset, Iris? My being Jayden's father or not knowing whether my interest in you is genuine or not?"

"Oh, no, you don't." She wagged a finger at him. "You don't get to turn this around on me."

Dane scooted closer to her until he was only inches away. "Yeah, I do. You're laying down all these edicts but I know you're not this woman. All angry and breathing fire. It's not who you are. It's not the Iris I've come to know."

"Don't presume you know me, Dane. You have no idea what I've been through."

"Well, what I see, I like," he responded. His eyes darkened even further until they were black as midnight. "And the feeling is mutual." When she attempted to shake her head, he called her out. "When we've kissed, you've responded. *Passionately.*"

Iris could feel a blush creeping up her skin.

"You've wanted me as much as I've wanted you," Dane responded. "You still do."

"I shouldn't have come here." Iris went to move away, but Dane's reflexes were lightning fast. He curled his fingers around her forearm and pulled her toward him, like an expert fisherman reeling in his catch of the day. She let him tilt her chin with those strong fingers and allowed his mouth to travel toward her in what felt like slow motion. Iris tried to hold back, but the minute their lips touched, she felt a flash of connection, so intense she released a moan of joy.

Dane's mouth explored hers with a thorough familiarity that had her mind racing. He plundered her lips until there was no oxygen left in her lungs and she had to draw back and suck in a breath of air. "Dane," she whispered.

Dane's chest tightened as he abandoned any thought of going slow. Instead, pure instinct took over and the kiss became hungry, hot and hard. He could hear the thud of his own heartbeat, especially when she pressed her soft curves against him. She was sweet and so responsive. He felt her nipples harden into pebbles through her blouse. He broke the kiss to lower his head and close his lips around one peak. He drew it into his mouth, making a wet patch on the shirt as he laved and teased the bud before moving on to the next one.

He wanted more of her. His hands crept lower until he found the waistband of her slacks. He slipped his thumb beneath them until he came into contact with bare skin. He felt her clench, but his intent was to keep going until he could caress her where she was surely hot and wet for him. The way she'd been wiggling signaled she was ready for a lot more, but when he went to move lower, she stopped him. Her eyes were hooded, but she just shook her head fervently, then moved to the other side of the couch.

"Iris, what's wrong? Did I move too fast?" Words were spilling out of his mouth because he didn't know how to react to the look of terror on her face. Had he misread her signals? He hadn't thought so. "Baby, what's wrong?" he asked again when he saw unshed tears on her lashes like morning dew on the leaves of a flower.

"I'm sorry. I can't." She started for his front door, but there was no way she could leave in the state she was in.

"Iris, please stay. I promise I'll keep away from you if that's what you want." He held up his hands. "Just stay. Please. You're in no condition to drive. You've already had one fright this morning. I'm sorry. I shouldn't have come on so strong."

"It's not you, Dane," she cried, and the tears that had been threatening began to fall. "We can't be involved. Not now. Not ever."

Iris continued to move away from Dane. If things had gone any further, he would have discovered the truth. Felt the scars from the accident that, no matter how many surgeries she'd had, wouldn't go away. She should have resisted, but the pull she felt toward him was strong.

"I won't apologize for kissing you, Iris," Dane said softly behind her, "because I wanted to, but I will say I'm sorry if I moved too fast. Why don't we put what's happening between us aside for a moment and talk about Jayden? It's out in the public now. We have to get in front of it and I'd like us to not be on opposite sides."

Dane had a point. She was way out of her depth in handling the kind of media attention she got today or would get in the future. Her feelings didn't matter right now. She—*they*—had to do what was best for Jayden. "All right, what would you suggest we do?"

"I'd really like to have a paternity test," Dane repeated. "I can get the test expedited and have results within twenty-four hours, if you're willing. I'll leave it to you on how best to tell Jayden what's going on. Even though I would love to be there when you did."

Iris noticed how soft his voice had become. It was as if he was speaking to a frightened horse needing cajoling. He didn't need to coddle her; she was much stronger than she looked. She'd already been through more pain than anyone could endure and come out on the other side. "It's best I speak to Jayden *alone*. And after that?"

"I release a statement to the press on how happy I am to have discovered my son and request privacy during this difficult time as we deal with our son's health."

"Do you honestly think it will be enough?" She didn't think the reporters she faced today were going to accept a simple press release.

Dane scrubbed his jaw with his hand. "Probably not. My team thinks we should do a televised interview with one of the major news outlets."

"*We*, meaning you and me?"

"Yes. If we present a united front, it could put some of the rumors to rest."

"Or spark more," Iris returned. "They could think we're an item and camp outside my house. I've heard the horror stories about the paparazzi. Is this really what you want for Jayden?" *For me*, she wanted to add, but kept herself out of the equation.

"No. But we don't have a lot of options here, Iris. However, I can help with securing your home and provide protection for you and Jayden."

"Is that really necessary?"

He nodded. "Please don't fight me on this. I *have* to do something. It killed me seeing the two of you besieged this morning without any protection."

"All right."

"To what?"

"To the paternity test and the security. I'd rather have someone there who is looking out for me and Jayden. But as for the interview, that's a no."

"Of course, I understand."

"I'm going to go now." She needed to leave because the air between them was still crackling with unresolved sexual tension. "Call me with the details for the test, okay?" She walked to the front door, and Dane followed behind her. She sensed he wanted to say more, but instead, he watched her leave. She was venturing into an unknown world she was ill-equipped to handle and she feared what was coming next.

Eight

"Dane, are you okay? We saw the news reports in Austin this morning," Fallon said.

It was well into the afternoon and Dane was still at home. He was in no mood to deal with the media and all the questions they would pepper him with. He was letting the initial dust settle when he got the three-way call from Fallon and Ayden.

"It looked like poor Iris was under fire," Ayden said, "and a bit stunned by the news you were Jayden's father. You didn't tell her your suspicions, did you?"

"No."

"Why not?" Fallon asked. "At least she could have been prepared."

"Please don't beat me up, Fallon. I feel guilty enough.

I left her open to be blindsided today and you can best believe Iris let me have it already."

"How'd that go?" Ayden inquired.

"Better than I'd hoped," Dane responded. "Initially she was upset with me, justifiably so, but after she calmed down and listened to reason, we were able to come to a consensus."

"And what was that?" Fallon asked.

"She agreed to the paternity test. She's taking Jayden after school to a private facility that will handle the test with absolute discretion. Iris will talk to Jayden and explain what's going on. I wanted to be there, but she thought it best she handle it alone."

"Wise move," Fallon stated. "Iris probably already feels like her entire world is spinning off its axis, but telling her son—"

"Our son," Dane corrected.

"Telling *your* son gives her some of that control back. I think you're going about this the right way. How are you planning to handle the furor over this news, though?" Ayden asked.

"I suggested an interview with one of the reputable networks. It would allow us to set the record straight and stop any speculation. But Iris disagreed."

"And what about you and Iris?" Fallon inquired.

Dane clenched his jaw. "I'm not ready to talk about that right now."

"It's okay, Dane. I was just curious. You have our support. We're here for you if you need us. Once you have the official proof Jayden is yours, we'd like to come visit if that's okay with you?"

Dane's mouth curved into a smile. "I have no doubts what the results will show," he replied, "and I would love that. Let's plan on it soon. It's time Jayden knows the other side of his family."

After he'd hung up with his siblings, Dane thought about Iris's reaction to their intimacy earlier today. One minute they were kissing and in the throes of a heated bliss and the next, she was pushing him away. Her response was way over the top and he wanted to understand why. Because Dane knew he wouldn't be able to keep his hands off her for much longer.

Iris ignited a hunger in him. Over the years, he'd grown cynical about women, especially the marital ambitions of the single women he encountered. Most of them bored the hell out of him. But when it came to Iris, she rocked him to his core and made him believe that maybe, just maybe, there *was* someone out there who could truly get him. Up until now, Dane thought he'd remain single forever. He hadn't seen many happy marriages. He certainly didn't count his parents' marriage as the epitome of happily ever after.

He'd suspected his father married his mother because she'd been pregnant with Fallon, tossing aside his first wife—Ayden's mother, Lillian—because Nora demanded it. Dane was certain he wasn't too far off the mark.

He was determined not to make his father's mistakes when it came to women. What was happening with him and Iris was so precious. She was a fierce mama bear, yet sweet and humble and oh so craveable. He would get to the bottom of her fears and whatever was holding her back because he didn't just want moments with Iris. He wanted all of her. *In his bed.*

After leaving Dane's, Iris planned to speak with Jayden. She wasn't relishing the idea, but it had to be done. Lord knew what kids were saying at school.

When the school day ended, Iris was waiting for Jayden outside of his classroom.

"Mommy, what are you doing here?" Jayden asked, walking toward her with his backpack around his little shoulders.

"I wanted to talk to you." Iris grabbed his hand. "Come with me." She led him to the principal's office, who'd graciously allowed Iris to use the room after she'd told her the situation. Iris nodded at the receptionist who motioned for her to go inside.

"Why are we going into the principal's office?" Jayden asked. "Am I in trouble?"

"No, honey, you're not," Iris said, closing the door behind them. "I need to talk to you about some important stuff."

"You mean about Mr. Stewart being my daddy?"

Iris swallowed the lump in her throat. There was no burying the lead in this conversation. "What have you heard?"

"Some kids at lunch showed me some video. Why is everyone saying that? You always told me I didn't have a daddy."

Iris sighed. She'd known this conversation wasn't going to be easy, but hadn't quite anticipated it being this tough. "I didn't lie to you, Jayden. Mommy would never do that. Usually mommies and daddies love each other so much, they make a baby together, but I wanted to have you so much that I used a medical procedure to have you."

Jayden frowned. "I don't understand."

"I know, honey, and I'm so sorry," Iris said.

She did her best to explain, but in the end Jayden was still confused. "We need to take a test to find out for sure if Mr. Dane is your father."

"What if Mr. Dane isn't my daddy?" Jayden asked.

Iris pressed her lips together. "Let's cross that bridge if we come to it, sweetheart. In the meantime, there's a lot of people who like Mr. Dane because he's in the movies and they want to know all about you, so we're going to play a game of hide-and-seek. We're going to hide from them, but they'll be seeking us out and asking questions. We're not going to answer them, okay?"

"Okay, Mommy."

Iris wrapped her arms around Jayden. She knew it was a lot for him to process and hated the position they were in. They were playing defense when they should have been playing offense. "C'mon, honey." She rose to her feet and grabbed him by the hand. "We're going to go out the rear entrance so no one sees us."

According to the receptionist, the press were now parked outside, hoping to catch a glimpse of Jayden, but Iris had switched cars with Shelly. When she'd called her sister at work, Shelly had been more than willing to help out. Iris couldn't believe she had to be so stealthy in order to ensure their privacy.

Dane had already texted her the testing facility's

address. They were expecting her, and when she and Jayden arrived, they were whisked right into an examination room. After completing a cheek swab, they were back on their way. Next she was headed to her parents' house. Iris knew they and her sister would want to know what was going on.

Pulling into the driveway, Iris turned off the ignition but didn't go inside.

"Mommy, why aren't we going in yet?" Jayden asked.

Iris released a long sigh. "No reason. I just needed to catch my breath." Within seconds, Jayden was bounding out of the car with no thought of whether they were being watched. It was Iris who glanced around the quiet tree-lined street looking for paparazzi, but there were none.

Jayden had already pushed the front door open and rushed inside when Iris made it up the front steps and into the foyer.

"Iris, thank God you've come over." Her mother, Carolyn, pulled Iris into the hug. She grasped Iris's face in both her hands. "Are you okay? I saw the news and, oh my god, I just can't believe it. Is it true?"

Iris stepped out of her embrace. "Where's Jayden?"

"He went to get some freshly baked chocolate chip cookies and some milk. I told him to do his homework while me and you have a serious talk."

Iris moved into the living room and glanced around. Her mother's taste was rustic; several antique pieces gave the room a cozy vibe. "Where's Daddy?"

"He's on his way home from work but he's called me several times asking if I'd heard from you."

"Well, let's sit," Iris said, sliding onto the comfortable microsuede sofa while her mom sat beside her. "I'll tell you everything you want to know."

"Is Dane Stewart Jayden's father? I mean, how is this possible? You were artificially inseminated."

"It's a crazy coincidence," Iris said.

"Are you sure, sugarplum?" a deep tenor voice said from the doorway. "Because I find in life there are no accidents."

"Daddy!" Iris popped to her feet and rushed over for one of his signature bear hugs. He wrapped her in his arms and gave her a gentle squeeze before setting her away.

"All right, girl. I'm here now." He took off the jacket he'd been wearing, hung it in the closet and joined them in the living room. "I left work because your mama told me you'd be coming over. Where's that grandson of mine?"

"He's in the kitchen, Charles," her mother replied, "eating cookies."

"Good. It will allow grown folks to have grown folk conversation." Her father sat down in his favorite reclining chair. "So, Iris, what in the hell is going on?"

Iris sighed and started over. "You know exactly what I know, Daddy. I went to a reputable doctor and was artificially inseminated. I got pregnant on the first try and nine months later, I had a beautiful baby boy."

"Where does Dane Stewart fit in this scenario?" her father inquired.

"Unbeknownst to either of us, it appears as if he was my sperm donor. He was a struggling actor looking for some serious cash and he was well paid for his donation. He'd forgotten the one time his sperm was used."

Her mother clutched her chest. "Do we have to keep saying that word?"

"Aw, Carolyn, don't be such a prude," her father chided. "Go on, Iris."

"He went about his life and I went about mine. Until Jayden's diagnosis. When I went on-air and pleaded for people to register as bone marrow donors, Dane's camp heard about it. He'd had a bout of bad press and needed to clean up his image. For him, registering was only supposed to be a feel-good story and he'd move on."

"Then what happened?" Her mother seemed as enthralled with the story as the rest of the country.

"Dr. Lee told Dane that he and Jayden were most likely related, but did he tell me?" Iris's voice rose. "No, he chose to keep that little bit of information to himself. Instead, he charmed his way into our life, by giving me his private number."

"And?" her father pressed.

"We started talking and he came over for dinner and spent time with me and Jayden."

"I knew it," her sister stated, storming into the house like a nor'easter. "You've been holding out on me."

"Where's my car?"

"Sitting in your driveway," Shelly said. "I took an Uber over here."

"Shelly, have a seat, please. Your sister was just sharing this bizarre tale of events," her father said. He turned to Iris. "So how did the press get wind of your relationship? I would imagine someone like him knows how to retain his privacy?"

"He thought he had it covered. Someone must have recognized him at the ice cream shop where we went after Jayden's PICC was inserted and alerted the media. Anyway, does any of it matter now? Reporters are going to be crawling through my and Jayden's life now and I hate it. We didn't ask for any of this."

"No, but you did choose to use a sperm donor, which has inherent risks," her father stated matter-of-factly.

"C'mon, Dad, not even you could have predicted my sperm donor would be a famous Hollywood actor," Iris responded.

Her father smiled. "No, I suppose not. And what about Dane? Does he want to be a father?"

"I think so. And in the meantime, while we get this sorted out, he's offered to give us a security detail to protect us from the media."

"You're going to need it," Shelly chimed in. "The Uber drove by your house on our way here. The television crews were swarming your neighborhood."

"This is all too much." Her mother stood and began pacing. "You already have so much on your plate with Jayden's illness. And now you add the press breathing down your neck. How are you going to handle it all?"

"One day at a time," Iris said. "I can't worry about what people think of me, Mom. Jayden comes first."

"From what you've said," her father replied, "sounds like Dane sees it the same way. I'd like to meet him."

"I dunno, Daddy."

"He's the father of my grandchild and has his sights set on my daughter. I darn sure want to meet him." Charles Turner puffed out his chest and Iris knew when she was beat. It was better to give in than to fight.

"Fine. I'll ask him."

"Good. Now come and get a bite to eat," her mother said. "I have some beef stew cooking on the stove."

Iris followed her parents into the kitchen and watched them and Jayden from the doorway. They were such a close-knit family with everyone looking out for each other. What was going to happen bringing Dane into the mix? Was she really ready for the changes ahead?

"You're going to wear a hole in the floor," Jason said, "if you don't stop pacing."

"Do you have any idea how I'm feeling?" Dane asked. "I've been in this mansion for twenty-four hours while the entire world gets to comment and Tweet on my life as if they had a right to. And what do I do? Nothing. Instead I have to listen to Whitney give me the business. Iris, who's in all likelihood the mother of my child, railed at me for keeping secrets and lying to her, when all I want to do is take her up to my bedroom and have my way with her. And then there's Jayden. He could be my little boy and he's suffering from a life-threatening illness. I'm all set to give him my bone marrow so he can get better, but I can't until he goes through debilitating chemo. Do you have any idea how inept I feel?"

Jason leaned back. "Okay, I think you must have

needed to let that out. And I'm sorry, Dane, if I've made light of this whole situation. It's just extremely unusual, ya know."

"No kidding. I'm living it, Jason."

"When will you know the results of the paternity test?"

"Within the hour. A courier will be delivering the results to both Dane and Ms. Turner simultaneously," Morgan chimed in from her position in the corner of the room. His assistant always seemed to be nearby when Dane needed her.

"Well, no wonder you're all wound up," Jason said. "Why don't you come with me to the gym? We can spar a bit and you can release some tension."

"I don't think that's a good idea," Dane said. "I'm in a foul mood and could hurt you."

"I can handle you, Stewart," Jason said. "C'mon, no sense in clock-watching."

Ten minutes later, both men had changed into sweats and were in the gym going through the paces. Dane hadn't realized how much he needed to relieve his stress until he took the first jab. Soon he and Jason were going toe-to-toe, with a jab here and quick punch there. It was exactly what Dane needed, so by the time he noticed Morgan in the mirror, hovering in the doorway, Dane was feeling good because endorphins were rushing through his veins.

Morgan held up the envelope and walked toward them. "The results are in."

Dane took off his boxing gloves and stared at the envelope for several seconds before accepting it. "Thank you."

"C'mon, Morgan. I'll buy you a Gatorade." Jason wiped the sweat off his brow with a towel from the nearby towel rack, and then they left Dane alone in the gym.

Dane's heart was beating fast because the contents of the envelope would change his life forever. The DNA test would officially set the record straight once and for all that Jayden was his son.

Sliding his forefinger through the flap, Dane pulled out the report. He wasn't interested in all the mumbo jumbo of how they arrived at the result; he wanted only to know unequivocally if he was a father. Scanning down the page, Dane found his answer.

Jayden was his son.

Nine

The driver pulled the SUV up to Dane's Venice Beach home a couple of hours later and Iris hopped out. Like him, she'd received the test results confirming he was indeed Jayden's father. Now Dane was going to be a permanent fixture in their lives because, knowing the truth, there was no way she would deny her son the chance to know his biological father. Although Dane hadn't been a part of Jayden's life from the start, he'd been prepared to donate his bone marrow. Had it initially been a media ploy? Yes. But he was a good man.

After reading the results, Iris had called her parents. They took the news in stride, as did Shelly, who thankfully agreed to come over and babysit so Iris could talk to Dane alone in person. But when she'd called him, Morgan had answered his cell. She'd informed Iris that

Dane had taken off on his bike. Morgan figured he'd gone to his Venice Beach house and suggested sending a driver so Iris could dodge the paparazzi. Then Morgan gave her the gate and key codes.

Iris had been surprised when three identical SUVs pulled up outside her home ten minutes later. Immediately, the news reporters sensed activity, especially when a beefy security guard got out of his vehicle, knocked on Iris's door and escorted her to one of the SUVs.

"Why three cars?" Iris asked as she got in.

"Subterfuge, ma'am. They won't be able to figure out which one has you." And with that, he closed the door and the SUV pulled from the curb.

An hour later, she was standing outside Dane's home. The paparazzi hadn't been able to follow her, but they were staked out at the gates of his beach house, desperate for a glimpse of Dane. No lights were on and it appeared that no one was home. Had Morgan gotten it wrong? Iris started walking toward the back of the house. Using the code Morgan gave her, she opened the side gate, which opened to a narrow alleyway that led to a private stretch of beach. The sight before her was spectacular. There was the Pacific Ocean in all its majestic glory, the sunset tinting the sky in various shades of orange, pink and purple. She could see why Dane liked coming here.

Toeing off her sneakers, she tucked them under her arm and walked in the sand. That was when she caught sight of him. Dane was standing outside on the terrace with a drink in his hand. He didn't appear to see her;

she could tell he was deep in thought. Iris understood why. She'd had nine months to prepare for Jayden's arrival. Dane had had less than two months to deal with impending fatherhood, but like it or not, it was here.

"Permission to come up?" Iris yelled to him.

Dane glanced down at her and blinked as if to make sure she wasn't a mirage. "What are you doing here? How did you get here?"

She smiled. "Morgan gave me the info. Now can I come up?"

"Of course." Dane quickly went to unlatch the gate leading up to his terrace. He opened it, and she walked up the few steps until she was standing in front of him. He was barefoot, and looked more handsome than ever in his usual outfit of T-shirt and jeans.

She offered him a small smile, and then reached inside her back pocket and produced a cigar. "Congratulations!"

Dane chuckled, but he accepted her gift with one hand, his tumbler of dark liquid in the other. "Thank you. I was outside watching the sunset. Do you mind?"

"Not at all."

She sat beside him on one of the loungers and together they watched the colors change on the horizon in silence. When it was over, he finally turned to her. "Before when I thought Jayden might be my kid, it was an idea, you know? But now—"

"It's different," Iris finished. "He's your son and knowing means you would do anything for him. Go to any lengths to protect him. Because you *love* him."

Dane nodded and if she wasn't mistaken she saw a

hint of tears in his eyes. "Yeah, I would. But it's also frightening because I don't want to mess up. I don't think I know how to be a father."

Iris chuckled. "Do you think I knew what I was doing?"

"No, but you chose to be a mom."

"You're right," Iris nodded. "I did. But listen to me, Dane. No one has some magical book that shows you how to be a good parent. We just have to do the best we can to love them and help them grow into good people."

"Thank you for the wise words. Now I don't know about you, but I'm starved," Dane said, heading toward the sliding glass doors. "You staying for dinner?"

"Am I invited?"

"As long as you can chop veggies, you are. When I got here, the fridge was already stocked. I thought I could whip up some pasta primavera. Maybe grill some chicken. How's that sound?"

"Heavenly." Iris kicked off her shoes and followed him inside, walking barefoot on the hardwood floors into Dane's killer beach pad. There was floor-to-ceiling glass that brought the ocean right into the home's open-concept main room. A cream sofa, ombré blue rug and azure chairs were in the classic white-and-blue seaside color scheme. The kitchen was fully equipped with a gas stove, spacious breakfast bar and state-of-the-art appliances.

"This place is amazing," Iris said. "And here I was thinking that nothing could top your mansion in the hills."

"I come here for privacy. And space when the world gets a little too claustrophobic."

Dane walked over to the fridge and pulled out boneless, skinless chicken and veggies before getting the pasta and sauce from the pantry. Iris didn't wait to be told what to do, opening several cupboards until she found the chopping board and some knives. They worked in tandem, cutting vegetables and chicken.

Eventually Dane uncorked a bottle of white wine and set about starting the grill. She followed him outside and watched him heat it up. "I never took you for a chef," she said, leaning against the rail.

"I'm not one." Dane laughed. "I know enough to get by and keep myself fed."

"I would think you'd hire staff."

Dane shook his head and placed the chicken on the grill. "I don't like all those people under foot. As it is, I have Morgan, Jason and Whitney and that's more than enough. They're always trying to get me to have a stylist, but that's not me. The only time I take fashion advice like that is for an awards show."

"Like when you won the Golden Globe. You must have been so excited."

"I was actually quite inebriated," Dane replied. "They keep the drinks flowing at that party. I like it best because everyone's more relaxed than at any other awards show."

"I suppose you want to win a golden statuette."

"What actor worth their salt doesn't?" Dane replied with a grin. "And maybe my last film is the answer and maybe it's not, but I'll never stop trying to get the brass ring. But you—you've stopped trying to find that special someone, Iris. Why?"

Her brows bunched together. "How did we segue from your career to my love life?"

"Because I want to learn more about you," Dane responded, turning the chicken over on the grill.

"I thought we were going to keep this about Jayden?"

"We are," Dane said, placing the tongs down on the grill's counter. He turned and looked into her eyes. "But there's something going on between us, Iris. And I want to explore it."

"E-explore it?" Her pulse quickened and the breath caught in her throat. His words had been spoken quietly, but the deep timbre of his voice could not be mistaken. She saw something in his dark, long-lashed eyes that made it impossible to tear herself away.

"That's right. I can't wait to have you in my arms again, so you can come apart."

Iris swallowed. "I'm going inside to check on the pasta." She knew she was being a chicken, but Dane's hungry gaze was making her overheat. After testing the pasta to ensure it was al dente, she busied herself in the kitchen by adding the vegetables to the cream sauce and taking out place settings for dinner. She was avoiding going outside and they both knew it.

Dane wasn't just any man—he was sophisticated, charming, skilled and, she was sure, very experienced in the bedroom. She wasn't a virgin, but it had been a long time since she'd been intimate with a man.

She reminded herself she wasn't sleeping with him, no matter what.

* * *

Dane returned to the kitchen several minutes later carrying the platter of grilled chicken. Iris had finished making the pasta, but it wasn't food that he was hungry for.

The jeans Iris was wearing skimmed her tush and made her waist look slender. And he liked her tank top and plaid shirt because they hugged her curves in all the right places. He was eager to explore what was underneath. He'd had only a taste of those delicious buds. Now he wanted the whole meal.

"Smells delicious," she commented. "The pasta and vegetables are ready."

"Hmm…"

"Are you listening to me, Dane, or ignoring me like your son does?" Iris said as she tossed the chicken in with the pasta, veggies and sauce.

Dane chuckled. "Does Jayden tune you out at times?"

"Sometimes when he doesn't like what I'm saying."

"Oh, I like everything you're saying," Dane countered, and watched Iris scurry to the other side of the counter.

"I thought you were starved. I know I am. I was on pins and needles waiting for the results to come in." Iris leaned over so Dane could scoop a healthy portion of the chicken and pasta primavera onto her plate. Then he dished some out for himself and they walked over to the dining room to eat their meal.

"What did you want the answer to be?" Dane said. "Were you hoping it wasn't true?"

Iris took a forkful of pasta and didn't answer right

away. "When I first found out there could be a chance, I was angry at you for keeping it from me, but the more I thought about it, the more I realized it would be a good thing for Jayden. Not just because you're his donor match, but because of all the things I hadn't taken account when I decided to have him. About Jayden *needing* a father." She reached for her wine and took a sip.

Dane nodded. "Thank you. It means a lot to hear you say that. I thought you might resent my role in Jayden's life."

"No, I'll champion it, because I want what's best for him, even if it isn't convenient for me." She continued tucking into her meal, avoiding his gaze.

"I understand. Being part of my world has its challenges. And if we go public and I acknowledge him as my son, the media frenzy will whip up around you. Are you sure you can handle it?"

"Do I have a choice?"

"You do," Dane said. "If you want me to, I'll deny I'm his father." He would do anything to protect his son and the woman he was coming to care for.

"I wouldn't do that to you or Jayden," Iris replied. "He needs you."

"Do you need me?" He took in how she was sitting too far away from him, and he wanted her closer, much closer.

"I need to get home," Iris said, wiping her mouth with a napkin and abruptly standing up. "It's late and my sister is watching Jayden. The driver Morgan sent for me has been kind enough to wait outside."

He glanced down at her plate. She'd eaten about half

her meal even though he knew she was enjoying it. She was running away like she always did.

She made it as far as the foyer before he caught up and stopped her. "Iris—"

She tilted her head, barely acknowledging him. "Good night, Dane." Her voice was low and faint. She started forward, but he put his hand on her shoulder, stopping her. She turned and he moved closer, allowing his hand to slide from her shoulder and fasten onto her arm. He felt her muscles tense as he drew her toward him. Time seemed to stop, and it was nothing but him and Iris.

Slowly, his mouth covered hers. She tasted like nectar sweeter than honey. She gave herself over to this moment of bliss and Dane took it, moving his lips over hers ever so softly and slowly. Dane kept his response measured. When he lifted his head, he said, "Stay with me tonight, Iris. I promise you, I won't hurt you."

She shook her head. "You don't understand—"

He didn't let her get another word out. Instead, he grazed his lips along the beautiful caramel skin of her neck and collarbone. Then with featherlight touches, he skimmed the curve of her breasts and felt them swell at his touch. He couldn't wait to touch his lips and fingertips to those stiff peaks until she released her husky cries like before. "Whatever it is, baby," he whispered, "whatever your fears, I promise you, we'll go as slow or as fast as you want."

He sensed her hesitation. Slipping his hand around the nape of her neck and cradling her head, he kissed her again, deeper this time. He wanted to make her wild with desire for him, to tantalize her with the promise of the sensual pleasure that awaited them.

And he did. Her arms slipped around him instantly, her lithe body, melting and twisting, pressing against him.

"Yes," she murmured. It was the sweetest word he'd ever heard. Not wanting to waste another moment, he lifted Iris into his arms and carried her upstairs to the master bedroom.

He set her down on his bed, cast aside the multitude of pillows to the floor and tugged her to him. Then he ran his hand from her neck to flank, urging her legs to open up to him. Careful not to box her in in case she decided to run for the hills, he slid his fingers through her hair, tilting her head until she could meet his kiss. Her entire body shivered, but instead of running, she moved closer, settling herself against him, causing a delicious friction against his hard erection. Oh, they were going to have a lot of fun tonight.

"I want you so much, Iris," he murmured. "Tell me you want me too." Because he couldn't wait to peel the clothes from her and rip his own off.

Her answer was to return his kiss, increasing the depth and pressure with her lips and tongue. Dane could feel her blossoming like a flower given water.

"I want you too," she moaned.

Iris couldn't believe this was happening. Dane had taken over her fantasies almost from the moment they'd met, but all along she'd pushed them aside. Now she was allowing this to happen. Although she was fearful of what Dane would find, perhaps it wouldn't be so bad with the lights off and the moonlight streaming in. Maybe…

He must have sensed her pulling away because he intensified the kiss, teasing and tracing her lips before plundering deep again. Her tongue sought his and she reveled in the heat between them. Her body was awash with sensation and she was mindless with delight. She'd never expected to feel this way, let alone with someone like Dane.

All inner protestations fell silent as she gripped his shoulders, pressing her body against his muscled chest and powerful thighs. He tugged the shirt down her shoulders and arms, revealing the cami she wore underneath. With his gaze on her, he cupped her breasts, grazing his thumbs over the peaks. Iris shuddered.

"You like that?" he asked, and when she nodded jerkily, he reached between them to pull the cami swiftly over her head, leaving her breasts bare to his gaze. She knew her breasts were small, but Dane didn't seem to care. He went lower, and Iris arched off the mattress when his mouth closed over her breast. She gripped his head, because she wanted to anchor him in place as he brought her dormant nerves to life.

He moved over to the other breast. His tongue swirled around her nipple while his mouth created a vacuum, sucking her in harder and harder. Iris felt herself tighten down below, but then he was moving past her breasts, placing lazy kisses on her stomach and teasing her navel as he went farther still. When he came to her jeans, he easily unzipped them and began sliding them down her legs. That was when Iris halted his hands.

"What's wrong?" Dane asked.

"I—I..." Iris faltered. How did she tell Dane she was damaged goods? That she wasn't like any of the beautiful starlets he'd been with? She didn't have to. Her jeans were already to her knees and Dane was looking down at the scarred, mangled flesh of her thighs. He glanced up at her with questions in his eyes she couldn't answer.

Then he finished removing her jeans. And instead of expressing disgust, Dane came closer. "I don't know what happened, Iris," he whispered, palming her face, "but I understand why you were nervous. You don't have to be. I think you're beautiful."

"You don't have to say that, Dane. You know the truth now."

"I know you're the sexiest woman I've ever had the pleasure to have in my bed. And I know that I've been thinking about you day and night."

"You have?"

He grinned devilishly "Will you let me love you tonight, Iris?"

She merely nodded, afraid to speak. She feasted her eyes on Dane as he shrugged out of his own clothes and joined her on the bed. That was when the fun began. Their bodies came together, skin on skin, and it felt so intensely intimate. But it was okay because all she saw in Dane's eyes were lust and hunger. A hunger for her.

So when he returned to where he'd left off and nudged her thighs apart, Iris was nervous. She nearly

bolted off the bed when she felt his warm breath near
her center and when he kissed her intimately, she let
out a long moan. He explored her with his tongue and
then added his fingers to her core, teasing and stroking, rubbing her slick heat. His intensity increased and
Iris heard a low moan and realized it was her.

Her thighs shook and she planted her feet on the
mattress, but his tongue and fingers continued pen-
etrating her. "Dane…" she sobbed. Her back arched
off the bed as a powerful orgasm roared through her.
Dazed, she collapsed backward on the bed.

Dane coaxed every last spasm from Iris until she
was flushed and bathed in a light sheen of sweat. Never
had any other woman tasted so good. He slid up her
body and they kissed again. It was deep and heady, and
this time Iris didn't hold anything back. She was an
active participant. Her hands drifted to his shoulders
and then skimmed his back and hips. He liked that she
was touching him and getting over her fear of intimacy.

Dane was curious about her injuries, but he wasn't
going to let that stop him from making love to her. And
when Iris moved her hand from his hip to curl her fingers around his pulsing arousal, he let out a hiss of air
between his teeth. Then she took one pebbled nipple
into her mouth, all the while stroking his length. He
was bewitched; his breath left his mouth with a whoosh
and his head dropped back on the bed.

Iris wasn't done. She climbed over him and had
her way with him. He wasn't surprised when he felt
her warm mouth teasing the tip of him. With gentle

licks and flicks of her tongue, she whipped him into a frenzy, so by the time her mouth closed completely over him, Dane bucked. But Iris held him down with her palms, all the while working magic with her mouth. Now a sheen of sweat covered his brow and he wanted, no, *needed* to be inside her.

Flipping Iris onto her back, Dane took over. He slid his finger inside her core. "You're ready for me, sweetheart," he said. As she closed her eyes, he reached for the drawer by his bed, grabbed a foil packet, ripped it open and sheathed himself. Then slowly, he slid inside her, but she was very tight. Dane sensed it had been a while and he gave her time to accommodate him. He brushed a tendril of hair from her forehead and looked down at her. "You okay?"

Her big brown eyes looked up at him and the trust there was a gift. "Yes."

"Good, because I don't want you to have any regrets."

"I won't."

Only when she began to wiggle her hips and relax into him did Dane begin to move. He slid in deeper, all the way in, and it felt sublime to finally make love to Iris. She put her arms around his taut shoulders, bringing him in closer.

"Please," she whimpered, clearly needing more.

So he drove deeper and she let out a moan, then another when he wrapped her calf around his thigh, pushing in farther, opening her up to him. Then he slowly began thrusting, setting a rhythm while their mouths fused, tongues twisting and dancing in a frenzy of need. Her inner muscles clenched around him and she clutched at him, her fingers digging into his back.

"Yes, yes…" she panted. He changed the pace to rapid thrusts and Iris met him stroke for stroke. When she cried out, it was a glorious sound that sent him crashing into the atmosphere as his body shuddered above hers.

A half hour later, Iris was feeling wonderful and more confident. Dane lay beside her, sprawled across the bed, asleep. They'd just made love and her mind and heart were full. Dane hadn't cared about her condition. He'd been gentle when he needed to be and eager when she'd wanted more. Iris hadn't thought it was possible she would ever find someone who could look past the physical. Dane Stewart could have any woman in America, but he'd *chosen* to be with her. It was a heady feeling.

But she mustn't forget herself. She glanced down at him. A real relationship with this man was unlikely but she could enjoy the moment. Tiptoeing from the bed, she found her jeans and retrieved her smartphone. Glancing around the room, Iris saw Dane's T-shirt and swiftly pulled it over her head and then went into the master bath to place a call to her sister. She wanted to check in on Jayden and make sure he'd had a good night.

Shelly answered on the first ring. "Iris? Are you okay? I was beginning to worry. You left hours ago."

"I'm sorry," she said. "I didn't mean to make you worry. I'm at Dane's."

"How did he take the news?"

Iris's mouth curved into a smile at the question. "He's excited to be Jayden's father, but understandably he was a little shook up by the weight of the responsibility falling onto his shoulders."

"I'm glad to hear it. When are you coming home?"

"I'm, uh, I'm…" Iris stuttered, trying to find the right words.

"Did something happen between you and Dane?"

"What are you talking about?" Iris's voice rose.

"Omigod, you're getting busy with Dane, aren't you?" Shelly didn't wait for a response. "Don't bother trying to deny it. It explains why we didn't hear from you."

"I can come home."

"I wouldn't," Shelly replied. "Enjoy him tonight, but I want all the details later."

Iris chuckled. "All right. Thank you, Shelly." She ended the call and opened the door only to find Dane standing buck naked in the doorway. Iris swallowed hard. "Hey…"

"Hey…" Dane gave her a winning smile that captured many a young woman's heart on the movie screen. "What are you doing in here? I reached for you and you weren't there."

Iris got a kick Dane was still thinking about her and not showing her the nearest exit. "I called my sister to check in on Jayden."

Dane sighed. "Of course you did because that's what mothers do. I should have been thinking about that, instead of keeping you away from him all night."

Iris could see the self-recrimination in his eyes and stepped forward, wrapping her arms around his waist. "Don't beat yourself up, Dane. I've had years of practice putting Jayden's needs before my own. You'll get used to it."

"I have a lot of catching up to do," Dane said. "How's our son?"

Our son.

Iris still couldn't believe those words. They shared a child together. "He's already in bed, so I didn't get to tell him good-night, but he's fine."

"Good." Dane walked her backward to the bed and they both came tumbling down onto the mattress. His hands framed her face as he looked into her eyes. "When do you think you'll tell him about me? I'd like to be there when you do."

"Tomorrow."

Dane nodded, and Iris could see he was worrying about Jayden's reaction. "Don't fret," Iris stated. "When I told Jayden there was a possibility you could be his father, he took it well. All we can do is be honest with him and how we intend to move forward."

"And how *do* we intend on going forward?" Dane asked.

Iris surprised herself when she circled her arm around his neck and brought his mouth back down to hers. "How about we think on that tomorrow?"

Ten

The next morning Dane didn't want to get up. He and Iris were in a safe cocoon as long as they were in bed, but as soon as they left, the real world would intrude on the precious time they'd shared together. They'd made love two more times last night and Iris had surprised him with her eagerness and utter abandon. There was nothing she wouldn't do for him or let him do to her. He'd been with lots of women over the course of his life. Since he was in his teens, his easy charm had made him a magnet for members of the opposite sex. But no one made his libido soar like sweet Iris Turner.

When she'd straddled him last night, he'd held on to her bottom, allowing her to rock against him. As she'd taken her own satisfaction, a low growl had escaped his lips. Every emotion had felt heightened. And when her mewls of pleasure turned into cries, he'd pumped upward to meet her, taking them both to a place Dane had never found before.

And now, knowing they shared a child together seemed only to further cement the growing feelings Dane felt for Iris. And Jayden had stolen his heart from the very first moment he'd seen him on television. Dane was looking forward to getting to know his son even though he'd sprung from very unusual circumstances.

He knew Jason, Whitney, Morgan and any number of people on his team were probably trying to reach him. But right now, all Dane wanted to do was be a man and a father.

Iris stirred from sleep and rubbed her hands over her eyes. She glanced up at him and blushed furiously. Was she remembering how many times he'd made her come and scream out his name?

"Good morning."

"Good morning. What time is it?" She sat up and reached for the duvet to cover herself.

"A little after eight."

"I should go." She made to move, but Dane halted her.

"Stay with me for the day. Then we'll tell Jayden together."

"Dane, there's no way we can go out together and not get caught. We tried that before and everyone knows you," Iris said. "And hell, with every media outlet running the story, they recognize me now too."

"Okay, you have a point, but don't you want to live a little?" If there was one thing he hated about being a celebrity it was being boxed in. "I want to spend the day with you and walk around like everyone else for as long as we can. And we can keep security nearby. How about it? Are you willing to walk on the wild side with me?"

"All right, let's do it."

Iris was glad she'd allowed Dane to convince her to escape the confines of his beach pad—even after an incredible shower together when Dane had gotten down on his knees and spread her thighs to pleasure her. Iris still colored thinking about the experience. Although she'd loved the morning and night they'd shared, it would be nice to get out together and have some fun. And that was exactly what they did.

Since she had no other clothes, Dane had loaned her a T-shirt that was huge on her. Iris had knotted it around her waist, showing off a little skin. Dane's eyes had gleamed with lust and she'd had to shoo him outside before they ended up horizontal again. Eventually, they made their way out of the beach house with Iris in a wig and Dane in a baseball hat and fake beard from one of his movies.

A dark SUV dropped them off near the beginning of the Venice Beach boardwalk. They held hands as they meandered the streets. Iris had a blast people watching. It was an eclectic mix, from mimes to musicians to jugglers. She loved the way the saxophonist played some old-school Kenny G and the way the street performers did some B-boy tricks. Along the way, she and Dane stopped for a hot dog and drifted into shops to look at the cool artwork on display. They even had their fortunes read. It had been very insightful: the woman had said big, life-altering changes were ahead for them.

That woman didn't know the half of it.

After leaving the fortune-teller, they found themselves in front of a bathing suit shop. Dane suggested they go in, but Iris hesitated. Why hadn't she discussed this last night? Because she hadn't wanted to. It had been different when it was just the two of them alone in bed. He'd made her feel invincible, but now that she was in public, it was a whole other story and her insecurities were kicking in big-time. She hated bathing suits because when she wore one, there was no way to hide her injuries. Anyone could see her scars.

"What about this?" A saleswoman came up holding a revealing high-cut one-piece, and Dane nodded in agreement. Maybe the models or actresses he dated would look great in it, but not her.

She shook her head.

"How about this one?" The salesclerk was trying to be helpful, but she was grating on Iris's nerves.

"Not my style." Iris stayed at the front of the store, fingering the wide-brimmed hats. She would need one to block out the sun and keep from getting freckles. If she stayed in the sun too much, she got a slew of them across her nose.

Dane sidled up beside her, holding the most revealing swimsuit yet. "I think you would look great in this one."

"Dane! Did you not see me last night?" Iris let out in a burst. "I would never wear this, or any of it." She motioned toward the racks of bathing suits and then rushed out the store.

He met her outside. "C'mon." He pulled her away from the shop toward the Hotel Erwin, which was a stone's throw away.

Iris was quiet as they went up to the rooftop lounge and settled onto a comfortable cushioned divan underneath an umbrella, a beautiful view of the Pacific stretching out endlessly in front of them. After a few minutes of silence, Dane finally ventured to bring up what occurred at the shop.

"I'm sorry," he said, hanging his head low.

"Why? It's not your problem," Iris responded bitterly. "It's mine."

Dane studied her and when she didn't say anything else, he asked, "Are you ready to share what happened with me?"

Iris knew she'd been unfair, but it was how she felt. "I'm sorry."

"For what?"

"Sniping at you."

"You had every right. It was incredibly insensitive of me to take you into a place like that. It's just that I don't see your scars, Iris. I only see you. Call me foolish or tell me I have it bad, but it's the truth."

His honest and sincere apology took the wind out of Iris's sails. "I'm hypersensitive about my body. You saw how I ran away the moment things started heating up between us."

"But I wore you down," he said with a sly grin.

"You didn't have to try very hard. I wanted you,

Dane. I still do. But you have to understand I'm never going to be comfortable showing off the lower half of my body. The car accident eight years ago changed me. It transformed my life and all the hopes I had for the future. It's why I did something as drastic as artificial insemination."

"Go on," he prompted.

"I'd been dating Mario. Your typical bad boy musician who liked to drink and have fun. My parents hated him, which of course only made him more appealing. So I broke curfew and did all the stupid things a young girl in love does. Until one day that bad boy drank and drove and wrapped his Ford Mustang around a tree with me in it."

"But you survived."

"Did I?" Iris asked. "I suppose, but I took the brunt of the impact while Mario walked away with only scratches. After the crash, the car caught fire, causing severe burns to my arms and thighs."

"But your arms…" He glanced down at them.

"I know you're thinking, 'How can that be?' Well, I endured countless reconstructive surgeries hoping to be my old self again. They worked on my arms. But after two years and many painful procedures, I just had to accept it—I was no longer the pretty girl I'd once been."

"Like hell you aren't! You're beautiful, Iris. Inside and *out*."

"Thank you for saying that, but I know what I see when I look in the mirror. And it's taken me a long time to accept who I am. Do I think I'm a monster anymore? No."

"Why would you say such a thing?"

"Because when I tried dating, a man told me I was, and after that I couldn't risk putting myself through rejection again. Until you came along."

Dane reached for her then, pulling her into a hungry, possessive yet masterful kiss, sending white-hot bolts of desire shooting through her. Without a second thought to where they were, she responded, kissing him back.

A discreet cough from a nearby waiter alerted them to the fact they were still in public. She looked up to see a man wearing a button-down shirt standing nearby. "Today was lovely, really," Iris said, "but—" she glanced down at her watch "—it's time Jayden learned the truth."

"You're right. It's time."

Dane was in a foul mood. After spending a leisurely day with Iris, enjoying all that Venice Beach had to offer and winding down on the rooftop lounge, they'd come outside only to be bombarded by questions from the press. Their day of being inconspicuous was over and now reporters were in full attack mode as Dane and Iris ducked into the SUV waiting at the curb. His security team had gotten wind of the crowd forming outside and ensured the vehicle was ready.

He didn't answer any of the questions. *Are you and Iris now a couple? When's the wedding?* And most importantly: *Are you Jayden's father?* He and Iris owed it to their son to hear the truth from them, not some muckraker.

The drive was slow, but eventually they made it to Jayden's school. Iris went inside without Dane because she didn't want the fanfare. As if that were possible. He'd already caught a handful of photographers lurking nearby.

Iris appeared several minutes later with Jayden at her side. He was dressed in khaki pants and a plaid button-down shirt and carrying a book bag. He looked like a little man.

One of Dane's security team opened the SUV door and Jayden's brow furrowed because he was surprised to see him. "Mr. Stewart?"

"Hi, Jayden." Dane scooted over on the back seat to make room for them. "I hope it's okay I came?"

Jayden nodded. "I suppose. It's just that kids at school are saying you're my daddy and if they see you picking me up from school, they'll think it's true."

Dane looked to Iris for guidance because he was tongue-tied. He was thankful when she stepped in. "How about we talk about it when we get home? Tell us about your day."

When the SUV stopped in front of Iris's house a half hour later, reporters swarmed the vehicle. Jayden glanced at his mother and then at Dane. "Why do all these people keep coming to our house?"

"We'll explain everything inside," Iris said.

As soon as the doors opened, the bodyguards were right there, preventing cameras and microphones from being shoved in their faces. Iris and Jayden disembarked first with Dane following suit. It was a melee, but eventually they made it inside.

Dane leaned against the door and watched Iris help Jayden with his belongings. He followed them into the small living room and waited. Standing by the mantel, he felt like a wood statue because he didn't know what to do. How was he supposed to tell a six-year-old boy he was his father?

"Come here, baby," Iris said, lowering herself to the sofa. "Sit with me." She patted the seat beside her and Jayden came over and sat down.

Jayden's eyes grew large. "Have I done something wrong?"

"No, no, of course not," Iris smiled. "You've been a good boy and I've proud of you for giving your lunch money to help a friend. Remember that test we took the day before yesterday?"

He nodded.

"We got the results back." Iris glanced over at Dane. "And well, the kids at school are right, honey. The tests showed that Mr. Stewart… Well… He's your father, Jayden."

Jayden looked at Dane standing there. "You're my daddy?"

A lump formed in Dane's throat and he forced himself to sit down and scoot over next to Jayden. "Yes, I'm your father." Dane finally said the words aloud to the most important person in his world other than Iris.

Jayden leaned toward him and swept his tiny arms around Dane's middle. Dane looked to Iris and saw tears swimming in her eyes, undoubtedly over Jayden's unexpected show of affection. He hugged Jayden as tight as he could. He'd never thought he would be accepted with open arms by the child, and it meant the world to Dane.

"I've always wanted a daddy," Jayden said. "I thought I wasn't normal like other kids."

Dane pulled back from Jayden slightly, but didn't completely let go. "You are normal. You may not have been conceived like other boys and girls, but there's nothing wrong with you. Don't ever let anyone make you feel less than." While it was true he was saying the words to his son, he hoped Jayden's mother would hear them too.

"You're squeezing me too hard," Jayden managed to eke out before Dane released him. "What does it mean?"

"It means I'm going to be a part of your life. You'll be seeing a lot of me."

"Are you coming to live here with us?" Jayden asked. "Are we going to live with you because you're rich?" He turned to his mother.

"It's not quite like that, Jayden," Iris responded.

"I don't understand. Other mommies and daddies live together."

"And you know some of them don't," Iris replied. "Like your friend Amy. Her parents share custody. She spends half her time with her mom and half her time with her dad."

Jayden frowned. "But I don't want to spend half my time with both of you. I thought you liked each other. You were kissing."

Iris chuckled. "I know it's confusing, honey. And yes, your dad—" she used the phrase for the first time and Dane's heart turned over in his chest "—and I do like each other, but we're still getting to know each other."

"So you could get married?" Jayden asked.

Dane interrupted his barrage of questions. "Not so fast, sport. I know you're excited and I am too, but your mom's right. We have to spend time with one another. I have to find out your likes and dislikes."

"That's easy. I don't like veggies and I like the color blue," Jayden answered.

Dane couldn't resist laughing at his son's forthrightness. "That's good to know, but your mom probably needs to get dinner ready and you probably have some homework."

"Not for much longer," Jayden said. "Once I get the transplant, I'll be out of school."

"That's definitely a plus. Iris, will you walk me out?" Dane stood up. "I'll be back soon, Jayden, and we can talk as much as you like."

Iris stayed behind with Jayden for a moment and then met Dane at the door in the foyer. "That went better than expected."

Dane nodded. "I thought it was going to be a lot harder, but he was so accepting." He felt his heart seize up in his chest. "I'm, I'm…"

"It's okay." This time it was Iris's turn to hug Dane.

Dane leaned and brushed his lips across hers. "I enjoyed last night and today, but it's only going to get crazier once I officially announce Jayden is my son.

Are you sure I can't convince you to come stay with me for a while?"

Iris shook her head. "This is Jayden's home. We won't be run out. Eventually, they'll get tired of the story and move on."

"But they'll be a nuisance."

"I know. And we'll deal with it."

"Thank you for including me in that 'we,'" Dane responded. With another kiss on her forehead, he opened the door and let his security guards and the crowd swallow him, taking him away from his son and the woman he was falling for.

Eleven

"So are you finally ready to talk strategy or is your head still in the clouds after blowing off me and Whitney?" Jason asked Dane later that evening when Dane summoned him to the Hollywood Hills mansion.

"Yeah, I am," Dane responded evenly, ignoring Jason's jibe.

"Good. Because while you were spending the day gallivanting in Venice Beach with your new ladylove, you were being crucified in the media," Whitney scolded. They were all sitting around the kitchen table while Morgan ordered some takeout.

"What are they saying about me now?" Dane asked. He was completely bored by the media's misrepresentation of the entire situation.

"They are calling you reckless," Whitney informed

him, "since you willfully donated your sperm without a thought to the consequences."

"Untrue," Dane stated. "As I recall, donations help infertile and same-sex couples, so I would beg to differ."

"Some outlets are stating this was all an elaborate media ruse."

"So what—I could vilify myself and put my sick child and his mother in front of a national audience? I don't think so."

Whitney held up her hands. "Don't shoot the messenger. I'm merely letting you know what people are saying so we can be prepared should you choose to make a statement."

"I plan on acknowledging Jayden Turner as my son," Dane stated. This was not up for discussion or debate.

"You realize your image as America's favorite heartthrob is toast?" Jason responded.

"I will *not* turn my back on my son in order to maintain people's false expectations or some fantasy they have about me. My boy is sick and I don't know how much time I could have with him. What if this bone marrow transplant doesn't work? I could lose him when I've only just found him." Dane jumped from his seat and walked out onto the terrace. The night was dark and there were no stars in the sky.

"We're not going to think like that," Morgan said, coming outside and handing Dane a beer. "He's going to get better because you've got great genes."

Dane smiled at his assistant. "Thanks, Morgan."

Over the last year, he'd found her to be loyal and reliable.

"Dinner will be here in a half hour. I'm going to head out, unless you need me?"

"No, I'm good, Morgan. Have a good evening." Dane returned to the kitchen to find Jason and Whitney staring at him.

"What?"

"I have never seen you like this before," Jason said. "You truly love that kid."

"It's true. I hardly know him, but he's my son."

"Then we release a statement of how overjoyed you are at your newfound fatherhood," Whitney said. "And that you intend to be a fully involved parent, sharing duties with Jayden's mother, whom you admire for taking care of your son during these formative years. You're excited to be a 100 percent match with Jayden, and you'll be taking time off to spend time with Jayden and prepare him and yourself for the transplant."

"Time off?" Jason inquired. "We're getting offers left and right for Dane. We can't take our foot off the pedal."

"You don't honestly expect me to be off shooting a movie while my son is fighting for his life," Dane said.

"But his mother is here. She's been taking care of him this entire time without any help from you."

"Jason, are you daft?" Whitney asked. "I know this is a shock to us all but there's no way I can spin it if Dane continues to be absent from his son's life. It would do more harm than good. Now here's the plan. We do an interview with your favorite anchor. And…"

Her voice trailed off before resuming excitedly. "We could even film your journey of becoming a transplant donor to help more people register. What do you think?"

Dane nodded. "Now you've got your thinking cap on, Whitney. I love it. Let's do it."

Whitney beamed with pride. "Thank you. I'll get right on this." She rose to her feet. "We'll talk tomorrow."

After she'd gone, Dane and Jason sipped their beers. Dane sensed his manager had something on his mind. "What's up?"

"Don't you think you're moving too fast? You hardly know this woman and now you're so entrenched in her life—"

"My son's life."

"Iris's too. Don't act like there's not something going on between you two. I know she spent the night with you last night."

Dane glared at him. "And how the hell do you know that?"

"Because I went to your beach pad and security refused to let me in. Said you had company and were not to be disturbed."

"I'll have to talk to them about being more discreet with my business."

"They didn't tell me who it was. They didn't have to. You have besotted fool all over your face. The pictures of the two of you today at the Hotel Erwin were all over social media. You don't need to be a genius to figure it out."

"Are you always this cynical, Jason?"

"I'm only looking out for your best interests."

"Then I would suggest you tread lightly, Underwood," Dane responded. Because there was no way Jason or anyone else would stand between him and his son. Or between him and Iris, for that matter. Speaking of, even though it had been only a few hours since he'd left them, it was time he checked in.

"How's this going to work?"

"Are you going to share custody with him? You get the weekdays, he gets the weekends?"

"Or just visitation rights and summer break?"

Iris covered her ears. She was having Sunday brunch with her family and they were firing questions at her left and right. She didn't have all the answers. She was still wrapping her brain around the fact that Dane Stewart was Jayden's father. And she'd had the best sex of her life with the man.

Dane had made a point of calling Jayden every night since they found out the truth last week. And just two days ago, Dane had come to Jayden's pretreatment. Jayden had lit up when he saw his father.

"Listen, guys," Iris said, taking a deep breath. "I don't know what's going to happen. Dane and I are taking it one day at time."

"With the statement and the televised interview coming up, Dane seems to be taking steps to solidify his position," her father countered. "You have to protect yourself, sugarplum."

"Dane would never do anything to harm Jayden."

"Or you?" her mother ventured. "I can see the stars in your eyes, Iris. Your father and I just want you to be careful."

"I need some air." Iris left them in the dining room. They were suffocating her with all their questions.

"Are you okay, sis?" Shelly asked from behind her.

"Yeah."

"I know they came on a bit strong, but they love you. As do I."

"I understand that, but is it so wrong for me to believe in someone again? To count on someone besides myself and my family to care for Jayden? You haven't seen the two of them together. They complement each other. Dane has a way with Jayden I haven't seen before and I want that for my son."

"No matter the cost to you?"

"What do you mean?"

Shelly shrugged. "I'm glad Dane has broken through the barrier you've had around yourself for years. That he sees the beautiful, sexy woman that you are. But I'm also urging you to be careful. He's an actor. A superstar, for heaven's sake."

"And I can't compete?"

Shelly shook her head. "No, but a lot of women throw themselves at him. There's always going to be temptation for a guy like him. Guard your heart."

Tears slowly made their way down Iris's cheeks. "It's too late, Shelly. I'm already in love with him."

"Oh, Iris."

"Please don't pity me, okay? His feelings may not be as strong as mine yet, but I believe he cares for me."

"Then bring him here to Jayden's birthday party. Let us meet him and see for ourselves the kind of man he is."

"You know the kind of man he is. He was the man who agreed to a transplant before he knew Jayden was his. If nothing else, trust that."

"I will."

"Jayden's birthday is coming up," Iris told Dane in bed the next evening at her home. He'd come over after his interview with Robin Roberts from *Good Morning America*. He'd chosen Robin because she'd been in Jayden's shoes with her transplant and understood why he wouldn't want to leave Jayden's side. She'd flown to Los Angeles for the interview. It had gone surprisingly well.

With the questions planned in advance, Dane had spoken candidly about his sperm donation, the reason for joining the bone marrow registry and finally his joy at discovering that not only was he a match for Jayden but Jayden was his son. Dane proudly claimed Jayden and welcomed him into the Stewart family.

The curveball came when Robin asked him about his relationship with Iris. He'd answered honestly, speaking of his respect and admiration for the mother of his child, but Robin hadn't taken the pat answer. She'd asked him about the images of them kissing and their day out in Venice Beach. Dane didn't want to attract more scrutiny to Iris, so he'd stated they were exploring a relationship.

Immediately after the interview, his cell phone

had blown up with Tweets, IMs and Instagram pics of women's devastation because he'd finally found love. Jason texted him angry-face emojis while Whitney stood enthusiastically behind the cameras giving him the thumbs-up signal. He was increasingly glad he'd hired her.

And now tonight, he and Iris were celebrating his media victory in the best way he knew possible. In her bed.

"Are you throwing a party?" Dane asked, gently caressing her cheek with his hand. "Do you think he'll be up for it?"

Jayden had started the chemo treatments and become increasingly lethargic. Dr. Lee had suggested he not return to school due to increased risk of infection. Despite the chemo and losing his hair, somehow his son still managed to smile each day. Jayden was a fighter. He took after his mother.

"Yes. Jayden has been looking forward to it. I'd hate to cancel. Plus, I already have something in the works, just family and friends."

Dane wanted to suggest inviting his family or at the very least his siblings, but he didn't want to be pushy. Iris was allowing him to be a father to their little boy. He wanted her and Jayden to be comfortable with his presence before introducing the entire Stewart gang.

Or maybe not the entire gang. Lord knows his mother hadn't been happy when she'd found out. Although they weren't close, he had FaceTimed with her and his father to share the good news they were grandparents again. Nora Stewart had been horrified over how Jayden was conceived.

"You donated sperm?" she asked. "Why would you do such a thing, when you could have asked us for money?"

"Because I was determined to make it in LA on my own two feet."

"Well, now you're saddled with a baby mama," his mother retorted.

He was annoyed by her response, to say the least. Why had he even bothered informing her? "I don't feel that way, Nora. Iris is a wonderful woman and if you're ever fortunate enough to meet her you'll treat her with respect."

"Of course we will," his father chimed in. "You know, this now makes Jayden our oldest grandchild."

"I'm not old enough to be a grandmother and now I hear you made me one before my time," Nora bemoaned. "Since he's old enough to talk, let Jayden know he can call me Mimi, because I refuse to be called Grandma or Nana."

"Duly noted," Dane returned. "Anything else?"

"When can we meet him?" his father asked.

"Soon," Dane responded. "Soon."

"Earth to Dane." Iris cut into his thoughts and he caught her wrists as she waved her hands in the air before his eyes. "Have you heard a word I've said?"

"Words? Hmm…" He leaned in and dragged his lips along her shoulder to her neck. Then he closed his mouth over the tender flesh there and sucked. He was pleased when he heard her whoosh of breath, and moved from her neck to her jaw until he returned to kiss her lips. Her eyes became heavy lidded, and she closed them. She trusted him with her body, and he didn't waste time undressing her, quickly tugging her nightie over her head. For him, it was pretty easy: rip off the boxers and he was naked.

Iris's eyes widened and traveled south to the mighty swell of his arousal. He wanted her panting underneath him, so he pushed himself back on his heels, pulled down her panties and discarded them. Then he was moving her legs apart to position himself between them.

"Dane…" Those were the last words he heard as he lowered his head and used his tongue, mouth and fingers to bring Iris to the peak. He licked, tasted and nudged, over and over again, alternating speed and pressure until he felt her quicken and she raced to the edge. Only then did he sheath himself with a condom and slide home. It took only a few final strokes for them to shatter into a million pieces, crying out each other's name.

Twelve

"Iris, I want to thank you so much for inviting the Stewart clan to Jayden's birthday party," Fallon said when she, her husband and son, along with Ayden Stewart and his wife, arrived at the Turner family home the following Saturday. The party hadn't yet started; they were an hour early. After making the introductions to her parents and sister, they were all sitting on the veranda.

"I want Jayden to know Dane's side of the family and you're his aunt," Iris responded. She'd secretly gotten Fallon's info from Morgan and called his sister. Iris sensed Dane wanted to ask her to invite them, but was afraid of stepping on her toes. But that wasn't possible. Jayden could never have too much love.

And the Stewart family had brought it in abundance.

It was supposed to be a small party, but they'd literally come with a delivery truck and unloaded box after box for Jayden. All his gifts were overflowing on the table in the backyard.

"What can I do to help?" Fallon asked when Iris rose to get them some refreshments.

Her mother and Shelly were already in the kitchen putting the finishing touches on the meal. Dane had ordered the birthday cake, which had been Jayden's only request. Dane had wanted to do something and she'd seen no reason not to let him. Morgan had brought the cake with her, telling Iris she was under strict orders to ensure the cake arrived in one piece. Iris had invited Morgan to stay for the festivities too.

"Not a thing," Iris replied. She looked at Fallon. Dane's sister could easily be a supermodel with her café au lait skin, hazel eyes and slender yet curvy body. While Iris had small breasts and narrow hips, Fallon had curves perfectly suited to her. She wore a wrap top and skinny jeans and looked like she hadn't seen a mop or a broom in her lifetime. "I want you to get to know your nephew. Plus you might want to keep an eye on your son— he's pulling out Mom's roses."

"Omigod!" Fallon jumped and rushed off to get Dylan, who was into everything. "Gage, help me… Please."

Gage was dreamy if you went for the tall, dark and handsome corporate type in trousers and a button-down shirt. Iris preferred Dane's rugged style. Gage wore his hair neatly cropped like he went to the barber weekly. His warm caramel-toned skin complemented his brandy-colored eyes. Eager to help his wife, Gage sprang from his chair and sprinted after Dylan.

Iris smiled. She remembered that age when Jayden was a Tasmanian devil and had to touch anything not bolted down. She was glad those years were behind them. She just hoped Jayden would be allowed to get the chance to grow up. A well of emotion surged through her and she could feel her eyes becoming misty.

"You okay?" a deep masculine voice asked from behind her. Iris turned to find Dane's older brother, Ayden, standing by her side. He appeared equally amused as she to see sophisticated Fallon and Gage being bested in a running competition by a toddler.

"I'm fine, just a little nostalgic." Iris sniffed.

"Time goes by fast, doesn't it? It's hard to believe I only connected with Fallon and Dane nearly two years ago. It seems as if I've known them forever."

"Was it hard gaining a family so suddenly?" Iris wondered if Jayden would be overwhelmed or excited by the prospect of so many aunts and uncles.

Ayden cocked his head to one side. "Not really. I'd always known they existed, and was kind of jealous of them at first. But I know now that it wasn't quite roses and sunshine for them either."

"I appreciate your candor," Iris said. "Thank you."

"You're welcome. So when is my nephew getting here?" Ayden inquired, glancing around. "I'm eager to meet the little fella."

"Dane took him for a haircut and a new outfit. He

wanted some father-son time alone. They should be here any minute. They'll both be surprised to see you."

Thirty minutes later, Dane couldn't believe his eyes when he saw his siblings and their spouses and children milling around in the Turners' backyard. He looked around until he found the person he wanted to thank—Iris. He'd had no idea when he stopped by Iris's earlier to pick up Jayden that she'd planned this.

The day hadn't started out great. Jayden hadn't wanted to go shopping, but once Dane told Jayden he could select his birthday outfit, his son had been thrilled. Jayden claimed his mother never let him wear what he wanted because it didn't match. They'd settled on jeans and a Puma T-shirt. Jayden was looking smart and hip. The most important thing for Dane was that Jayden was happy. It was why they'd kept the birthday party a secret from everyone except family and Morgan who was quickly becoming like a baby sister to him.

But when they left the store, the trouble started. They were mobbed by a large crowd eager to get their first look at Dane and his son together. The store manager had to usher them through the back door to leave and get back in time for the party.

"Jayden, c'mon. I want you to meet your aunt Fallon." Dane rushed over to his sister. She met him halfway, and he hugged her tight. He didn't realize how much he needed his family until they were here with him.

"It's okay," Fallon whispered so only he heard her. "Your big sister's here."

He squeezed her tightly one more time before letting her go. He shook Gage's hand, kissed his sister-in-law and gave his big brother a one-armed hug. "I can't believe you all kept this secret from me."

"Trust me, it wasn't easy," Gage said. "Every time Fallon talked to you I thought she was going to spill the beans."

"Hey, hey, I know how to keep a secret."

Dane crouched down to Jayden's height. "I'd like you to meet the other half of your family, Jayden. This is my sister, Fallon, and brother, Ayden. They're your aunt and uncle."

"Pleasure to meet you," Jayden said formally.

"And this is my husband, Gage." Fallon kneeled down, looking into Jayden's eyes as she spoke. "So I guess that makes him your uncle Gage and Ayden's wife, Maya, your aunt Maya and then there's Dylan running around here."

"That's a lot of names to remember." Jayden scrunched his face.

"It's not a test, Jayden," Dane said. "In time, you'll remember their names."

Jayden nodded. "Is that all my gifts over there?" He eyed the mound of wrapped presents sitting on the table.

"All for you, nephew," Ayden replied. "We couldn't come empty-handed."

"You guys are the best!" Jayden ran to the table.

Dane stood and watched Jayden shake each gift, trying to figure out what was inside. "He's awesome, isn't he?"

"It's hard to believe he's sick," Maya said quietly.

Dane glanced at his sister-in-law. "I know. You'll be able to tell as the afternoon progresses. He'll become more and more tired. He gets drained from doing normal activities."

"How long before he can get the transplant with your bone marrow?" Fallon inquired.

"A few months. He's going through the pretreatment chemo first to wipe out his immune system. Then he'll get the transplant and have to stay in the hospital for months to ensure he doesn't reject my bone marrow."

"I'm sorry Jayden has to go through this," Fallon commented.

"My son is strong." Dane glanced across the yard at Jayden. He'd seen their resemblance from the start, but as time went on, he'd seen a resilience in Jayden that reminded him of Iris.

Fallon smiled when her gaze connected with his. "Your son."

"Who's ready for some lunch?" Iris yelled from across the yard. "Come and get it!"

"Isn't she amazing?" Dane said aloud to no one in particular. Dane couldn't get enough of Iris. They'd made love twice this morning and he was still excited about being with her tonight. "I love that woman!" The words were out of his mouth before he realized he'd said them.

Dane glanced at his siblings and they were both looking back and forth at one another. He laughed nervously. "I didn't mean that how it sounded. It's just she's so thoughtful, bringing you all here."

"Sure, bro," Ayden said, patting him on the back. "That's exactly what you meant." He smirked as he walked off with Maya toward the picnic table laden with fried chicken, potato salad and a fruit-and-veggie tray. Gage scooped Dylan up in his arms and walked off, leaving Dane and Fallon alone.

"C'mon, sis." Dane stepped farther away from the group. "No need to give me that look. It was a slip of the tongue."

"Who are you fooling, Dane? Certainly not me, but maybe yourself. I saw the way you looked at Iris when you realized she'd pulled off this surprise for Jayden's birthday party. You were touched. *Deeply.*"

"I'm attending my son's birthday party for the first time. Of course I'm affected, Fallon. I never thought I was going to be a dad—parenthood wasn't in the cards. That was going to be something only you or Ayden did. But this, this came out of nowhere and blindsided me, but in a good way, ya know?"

Fallon nodded. "I do, so I'm going to give you a piece of sisterly advice and you can do with it as you like. Leave the past in the past. Mom and Dad don't have the perfect marriage. So what if they aren't madly in love? That doesn't mean true love can't exist. You can be happy, the three of you. You, Iris and Jayden, as a family. Don't rule it out."

She left him standing there, watching her as she walked away. Was she right? Was he projecting his misconceptions about love and marriage onto him and Iris? He'd thought he came to the table with a clean slate and they had only Iris's insecurities to face, but perhaps she wasn't the only one who needed to heal. He was afraid to admit to Fallon and maybe even to himself…that he was in love with Iris. It scared the living daylights out of him, because he'd never been in love. Until recently, he didn't even know what it was. All he had to go by was his parents' train wreck of a marriage. But seeing Fallon and Gage and Ayden and Maya gave him hope that love was worth the risk to his heart.

"I'm impressed," her father told Iris when she went into the kitchen to top off the beverages.

"With what?" Iris asked.

"Dane and his family. Considering he's famous and they're rich, they're down-to-earth people."

"I told you, Daddy."

"Yeah, you did, but I had reservations," he replied. "But seeing how Dane is with Jayden and how he looks at you has made me realize I misjudged him."

"How so?"

"He's an actor, Iris. I thought he was snowing you, but I can see he really does care for you both. And if I'm not mistaken, I'd say the young man has stars in his eyes when it comes to you."

"Oh, Daddy. There's probably something wrong with your eyesight."

"I know what I saw. I haven't seen you light up this way in years, baby girl." Her father stopped her from adding bottled waters to her tray. "I'm happy to see that spark in your eye. After the accident, you lost it, and I thought you'd never get it back. But Dane—he's the reason, isn't he?"

Iris shrugged off his question. She wasn't ready to talk about her tender feelings for Dane aloud to anyone, at least not yet. "Dane coming into our life has brought us so much joy, especially because Jayden has such a long road ahead."

"C'mon." Her father nodded his head toward the terrace. "Let's go make this a birthday Jayden will always remember."

"You go on." Iris handed her father the tray filled with drinks and watched as he left the room. "I'll be there in a minute."

Her father's words had reminded her of Jayden's illness. If he couldn't withstand the treatment or if the stem cells from Dane's bone marrow didn't take, this could be her last birthday with him. The sadness Iris had been keeping at bay washed over her, and she covered her mouth with her hand.

"Iris?"

Dane's voice brought her back to reality and she quickly brushed the tears away from her cheeks. Taking a deep breath, she turned around to face him.

"What's wrong?" Sensing her distress, Dane immediately came forward.

She sighed. "I was so happy and then it dawned on me, Jayden might not—"

Dane reached for her and grabbed her by the shoulders. "Don't say it, Iris. Don't even think it, okay? You have to stay positive. Jayden is *going* to pull through this."

"How can you be so sure?" The odds weren't in their favor. She would never forget when Dr. Lee had first shown her the graphs and charts of Jayden's life expectancy if he didn't get a transplant. It had been frightening.

"Because…he's a fighter like his mom and dad."

Iris couldn't resist a small smile forming on her mouth. "How is it you know exactly the right thing to say to keep me from being a Debbie Downer?"

"Because I have bucketloads of charm."

Iris chuckled and looped her arm through his. "You're so arrogant, but I adore you." She glanced up at Dane. She'd nearly said the *L* word but caught herself in time. They weren't in a place to have *that* particular conversation but it was coming. Sometime soon.

"Happy birthday to you,
Happy birthday to you,
Happy birthday, dear Jayden,
Happy birthday to you."

Jayden's blended family sang to him. Dane was so grateful Fallon and Ayden had made the trek to LA. Being here with Iris and her folks along with his made the moment more poignant, because Dane hadn't felt this way about family in a long time. Was he getting soft?

"Make a wish," Iris said.

Jayden closed his eyes and then blew out his birthday candles on the Transformers cake Dane ordered. Dane had made sure Morgan had found the best baker in all of Los Angeles because only the best would do for his boy.

Dane laughed when his nephew stuck his finger in the icing. "Dylan!" Fallon reprimanded him, but he didn't seem to care. He'd already gotten what he wanted and was licking his fingers.

"Are you ready for one of those?" Dane asked Ayden, who was a couple of feet away.

"Yeah." Ayden nodded. "I actually think I am."

Dane pulled him aside. "You know, it's a lot harder than it looks. I've been getting a crash course on fatherhood."

"I know, but I'll have the next six months to prepare."

Dane glanced up at his big brother. "Are you saying...?" He let the words trail off because the goofy grin on Ayden's face was a dead giveaway. "Have you told anyone yet?"

"Naw, man, you're the first. We were waiting until the second trimester, but Maya's nearly there and I've been dying to tell someone."

"Congratulations." Dane pulled Ayden toward him and they embraced. "I'm happy for you both."

"Thank you, thank you." Ayden glanced behind him and when he laid eyes on Maya his entire demeanor changed. Dane wondered if that was how he looked when Iris was around. "I'm a lucky man. I'm so thankful she came back to Austin. If it hadn't been for Maya coming home for her niece's baptism and her mother's cancer treatments, I may have never seen her again."

"How is her mother doing?"

"Thanks for asking. She's in remission," Ayden said. "It was touch and go there for a while, but she pulled through. It even brought Maya and her sister, Raven, closer."

"Adversity will do that," Dane responded. He glanced at his son, who was devouring a piece of the chocolate cake. Icing was all over his face, but he looked content.

"He'll be okay."

Dane looked up at Ayden. Though they'd reconnected two years ago, they hadn't seen each other much. Lately, however, their bond was becoming stronger. "Thanks, Ayden. I appreciate it."

"Before I forget to ask you… Your assistant, Morgan. Who is she?" Ayden inquired.

"A film school dropout who is working for me. Why?" Dane inquired.

Ayden shrugged. "I don't know. There's something familiar about her."

"I'm sorry to break up this bromance," Fallon called out as she said her goodbyes to the Turners, and Iris and made her way toward them, "but we're going to head home."

"Back to Austin?" Dane asked with a frown. "You just got here."

Fallon stroked his cheek. "And we'll be back. Now that we've met our nephew and Iris, you're going to be seeing a lot more of us. Maya tells me she has a doctor's appointment she can't miss tomorrow."

Dane smiled knowingly. "Of course. Thank you all for coming." He squeezed Fallon in a tight hug. "Gage." He shook his brother-in-law's hand. "Take care of my sister."

"Always," Gage responded.

When Maya came over to him to say goodbye, Dane hugged her close and whispered, "Congratulations."

"Ayden Stewart." Maya turned her full gaze on her husband. If it was possible for a grown man to tuck his tail between his legs and run, Ayden would have done it right then. He had guilty written all over his face. Maya smiled at Dane. "We'll see you again soon."

"Today was fantastic, Iris," Dane said once they'd put an exhausted Jayden to bed. On the way home, he'd talked incessantly about the party, all his gifts and his new aunties and uncles. He'd even taken a shine to Dylan, who'd followed him around like a puppy dog.

And they hadn't even had too much trouble with the paparazzi. When they'd arrived at Iris's, a few tabloid reporters had yelled happy birthday to Jayden, and one had asked if having Dane as his father was the best birthday gift. Dane wanted to deck him, but knew the best approach was not to ignore him and not feed into the mania.

Now Dane and Iris were going to bed. Dane had gotten rather used to spending the night over at Iris's. At first, they'd been worried about how Jayden would react. They needn't have bothered. When Dane had come out of the bathroom wearing his boxers one morning, Jayden merely said, "Hey, Daddy," and went back into his room. It was the first time he'd called him that and Dane had been overjoyed. Iris had still worried about the impact on Jayden. But over bowls of cereal later that morning Jayden had told her he liked having Dane around, saying he felt safe. And that was that. Dane began staying over more often.

"You really enjoyed it?" she asked, smoothing hand cream on after brushing her teeth and removing her makeup.

"Couldn't you tell?" Dane asked, pulling the covers back. "I was touched you included my family in Jayden's birthday celebration. And better yet, you managed to keep it a surprise from me. *You and Fallon*."

Iris rubbed her hands together. "We were great co-conspirators."

"Yeah, you were," Dane said. His fingers clamped down on her arm and hauled her down onto the bed with him. He'd already undressed to his boxers, which he didn't intend to keep on for long. He lowered his head and she accepted his invitation readily, allowing his seeking tongue entry into her mouth. Her kiss gave him life when for years he'd been a wasteland Unfeeling, emotionless, not allowing another person in. But Iris changed all that. She gave him hope and the promise of so much more.

His hands skimmed the nightie she wore. It was a piece he'd bought for her after seeing it in a shop on Rodeo Drive. He'd thought it was beautiful and delicate, just like Iris, and purchased it. When he'd presented it, Dane loved how Iris had blushed like a schoolgirl. It was one of the many endearing things he loved about her. And so he continued his languid exploration of her mouth while his hands eased over her curves. He didn't care about the scars. Did he know they were there? Yes, but he no longer saw them. *Only Iris*.

When he lowered the strap of her nightie and placed his mouth over one breast, she shuddered in his arms, arching her back. His teeth tugged at her nipple while his hands dipped to the backs of her knees. Finding the edge of the nightie, he lifted it by the hem over her head, so he could feast his eyes on her incredible body. He groaned when he saw the dark curls of her womanhood and immediately his erection swelled. That was what Iris did to him: she made him hot and eager. He reached for the nightstand and after donning protection, thrust inside her, filling her completely, leaving no space for anything but him. He drove into her purposely, before withdrawing, only to surge in again.

He couldn't stop the overwhelming force that was lifting him, higher and higher, as he thrust inside her. Iris moaned her appreciation and Dane lost himself, coming apart with a deep guttural cry.

"Iris, I..."

Words were on the tip of his tongue, but he didn't set them free. Instead, he shuddered into her, which prolonged her release and sent them both hurtling into space.

Thirteen

The next few weeks flew by for Dane. Every other day he was going to the pretreatments with Jayden and Iris And each day, he could see some of the vitality drain from Jayden's face.

Meanwhile, he and Iris's relationship bloomed. He took her to his favorite barbecue joint, where she dug into the meat platter full of ribs, smoked sausage and chicken and licked the sauce from her fingers.

"Delicious," she'd said, and he couldn't resist taking her fingers into his mouth and licking the sauce off.

Yes, it is, Dane had thought.

He took her to a Los Angeles Clippers game and secured much sought after tickets to a Beyoncé and Jay-Z concert. They needed these stolen moments to help deal with caring for their sick child. Of course, their outings brought much fanfare with the entertainment shows commenting on each date and what Iris was wearing. Surprisingly she took it in stride. It helped that Dane had hired Iris a stylist for such occasions to ensure she felt comfortable. She'd even convinced Dane to attend *Hamilton* in New York over a weekend while Shelly babysat. He knew it was all the rage, but he could have had a V-8. He loved being with Iris, though. Loved having her in his life…

And he loved making love to her. Sometimes it was fast and furious with no time for foreplay. Other times it was slow, with Dane making every kiss, every stroke, sweeter and longer than the last. Tonight, however, was going to be different.

He and Iris were attending a Friday evening premiere for one of his acting buddies. His team had been involved in every step, including selecting their attire to ensure they complemented each other. Morgan hired a stylist and hair-and-makeup team for Iris to ensure she looked her absolute best. In Dane's eyes, Iris was already perfect and didn't need a makeover team. Although she hadn't said anything, he suspected Iris was nervous about the appearance and wanted to give her as many tools as she needed.

Iris had arrived at his Hollywood Hills home a couple of hours ago. Her parents were babysitting Jayden so they could have a night out on the town. They'd been great, always supportive and willing to lend a hand if Dane and Iris wanted some alone time. He wished he could say the same for his parents; they'd yet to make an appearance to meet Jayden, though they had sent him a birthday gift.

"I have your diamond cuff links," Morgan called out, disturbing his thoughts as she knocked on his open bedroom door.

"Thanks, Morgan." Dane took the pieces from her. "These will work well for tonight. What would I do without you?"

"I don't know. I think you'd kind of miss me."

"Having you here is like having the kid sister I never had," Dane said. A weird look came across her face, but it was fleeting and quickly replaced with a smile.

For Dane, the premiere was one of endless events he'd attended to keep his name out there. He also gave back to a number of charities, which meant he frequented hospital fund-raisers, gallery openings and galas. Dane could care less about the Hollywood elite or crème de la crème of society, but he recognized the importance of nights like this.

Once he'd showered and dressed in a black suit with a black shirt and tie, Dane was ready for the evening. Morgan whistled when he came down. "You look great. I'm sure Iris will be pleased."

"I certainly hope so," Dane replied with a smirk. "'Cause I certainly wasn't doing it for you."

"This is a very big deal," Morgan said. "Your first official appearance as a couple. Are you ready for the brouhaha?"

"Iris and I have been out many times."

"But not with the fanfare of attending a movie premiere where all the world's press will be in attendance," Morgan responded.

"I'm not worried. Iris will be great."

"I don't know if I can do this." Iris nervously paced across the plush carpet of one of Dane's guest bedrooms. "I mean, do I look okay?" She glanced down at the sparkling white floor-length gown. Four spaghetti straps were asymmetrically located across her shoulders, dipping in a V at her cleavage. The stylist had teamed it with simple black pointed heels, a sparkly clutch and large black shades.

"You look fabulous, Iris," Whitney gushed. She was here for moral support.

"You don't think it's too bold?"

"It's attention grabbing," Whitney stated, "and that's what we want. This is the public's first chance to get a genuine look at you all glammed up, so we want them to know you're proud to stand at Dane's side. Your hair and makeup are flawless." She gave the hair-and-makeup artist a thumbs-up.

"Thank you." Iris's normally wavy hair had been roller set and she now had big curls touching her shoulders. Add her scarlet lipstick, and it was a very 1920s glam look.

"C'mon, I'll take you downstairs. I'm sure Dane is eager to see you." Whitney propelled Iris toward the door. Navigating the sweeping spiral staircase in four-inch heels wasn't easy. Iris breathed a sigh of relief when she made it to the living room in one piece. Dane and Morgan were already there along with a couple of his bodyguards.

A large grin spread across Dane's face when she walked in the room. The look of searing heat he gave her caused everyone else to fade from existence. He held out his hand to her and Iris walked toward him. She gave him her hand and he kissed it. "You look stunning."

"Hearing you say it, I believe it," she whispered.

"You ready to get going?"

She nodded.

"All right, folks, we're heading out." Dane led Iris toward the foyer. "And might I suggest you all be gone by the time we get back?"

Iris blushed as she headed outside with him. It was a warm, pleasant evening and she didn't need a wrap. She slid into the limousine and Dane joined her.

"Don't be nervous." He patted her thigh.

"Easy for you to say. You won't have the entire world looking at you waiting for you to mess up. It's why I agreed to the makeover to begin with."

"Is that really what you think?"

Iris turned to give Dane an incredulous stare. "C'mon, Dane. I'm not that naive. I know your team." She motioned with her thumb toward the mansion they were pulling away from. "I know I'm not your type."

She'd seen the type of women Dane dated in the past. Sophisticated and poised, with money and opportunities to spare, they'd probably never had a day of uncertainty in their entire life. Iris wasn't that woman. Maybe she could have been if it weren't for her accident. As it was, she'd asked for privacy when it had come time to dress. Her scars were no one's business but her own.

"*I* don't care about any of them. The only people who matter are in the back seat of this limo. Me—" he pointed to himself and then to her "—and you."

That was easy to say, but did he really believe it? Iris looked away, but Dane tipped her chin to face him.

"I mean it, Iris. I've always been upfront and honest with you. Don't doubt that and let anyone poison what we have. Don't doubt us. If you do, then they win."

Iris nodded and tried to keep the tears that were threatening to fall at bay, but in the end a single drop trickled down her cheek, and he wiped it away with the pad of his thumb. Then he leaned in and softly kissed her. It was sweet and poignant and did the trick to settle her nerves.

She gave him a tremulous smile and before she knew it, they were at their destination. Maurice, one of their bodyguards, turned around to face them. "It's time."

"You ready?" Dane asked, and Iris nodded.

Then Dane was sliding out of the limo. From her position, all she saw were flashes of light. Dane was in front of a big spotlight being photographed by tons of news media outlets. Iris was unprepared for the near frenetic energy surrounding the red carpet, but she placed one high heel tentatively on the pavement, and Dane took her hand, ostensibly to help her out of the limo. All the while cameras continued to flash in her face.

Iris smiled as best she could, reminding herself this wasn't real. On any given Sunday she was in her pajamas watching the red carpet for the Oscars or some other Hollywood award night. Instead, tonight she was with Dane as he waved at his screaming fans, who held up signs with his picture and yelled they loved him.

Dane bent his head and placed a kiss on her cheek and the crowd went wild. Reporters were yelling questions from all angles. Dane answered he was excited to have Iris on his arm tonight and they looked forward to a great movie.

In the end, the movie was a complete dud, but Iris had never had more fun. Once she allowed herself to relax, she found celebrities were like everyone else with their own fears, insecurities and quirks. She and Dane stayed long enough for him to wish his friend luck at the box office before they departed for a late dinner.

Instead of going out the front where Iris was sure the press waited, Dane led her out a side entrance to his SUV. "When did you arrange this?" she asked, giving him a sideways glance.

"I gave the fans what they wanted at the beginning of the evening," Dane said. "The rest of tonight is for us."

"I like that. I like it a lot." She'd worried unnecessarily because in the end Dane was so thoughtful and cared about her needs. Something about him drew her closer and it was more than the powerful lust they shared, though they had that in spades. It was more. It was the tingle in her belly every time she saw him. It was the sensation galloping through her like wildfire when he touched her. It was the fireworks she felt when they made love.

It was love.

Fourteen

"I'm thinking of asking Iris to marry me," Dane told Jason when they met up for a meeting that Monday morning. Jason had asked Dane to come to his office because he wanted to talk shop with no interruptions. And that was fine with him. It gave Dane time to go ring shopping and find the most exquisite and unique piece he could for a special lady.

"You're what!" Jason bolted from his seat and came around to face Dane. His agent was in his customary dark suit and tie, wearing designer loafers. "Are you mad?"

Dane stepped back and glared at him. "What's your problem, Underwood?"

"You're a star, Dane. A bankable Hollywood sex god. It's what we've sold you as for years. It's been your calling card. Now suddenly you want to flip the script?"

"I'm not the first A-list actor to get married," Dane responded evenly, "and I certainly won't be the last. My marrying Iris won't change my popularity."

"Why are you doing this?" Jason asked incredulously. "Out of guilt? Because you haven't been there for your son? Out of some misconceived notion of responsibility? You weren't responsible for Iris choosing to get herself knocked up by a sperm donor."

Dane shoved Jason against the desk and bore down on him. "Don't you dare speak ill of Iris. Not only is she the mother of my child, but she's a damn fine woman. You have no right to judge her, Underwood, especially considering some of the things you've done."

Jason's eyes narrowed. "Are you really going to turn on *me*? On me? After everything I've done? I made you into a star."

"And you got paid handsomely," Dane responded. "Don't act like it was altruistic on your part. You've benefited from my success."

"And I've been like a brother to you, more than your own family," Jason countered.

"Do you think that gives you the right to tell me what to do?" Dane yelled. "Don't get it twisted, *Jason*. At the end of the day, you're my manager and agent. And I thought you were a friend, but I'm beginning to wonder if all you care about is your own best interest. But guess what? This is *my* life. I get to choose. Not you. Not the press. Not the general public. You got that?" He poked his index finger into Jason's chest.

"Fine. Do what you want. Throw away your life. Just don't cry to me when it needs fixing because you've screwed yourself."

"I'll remember that and take my leave before I say something I can't take back," Dane said. He started for the door and then turned around. "Why did you call me here anyway?"

"I thought you might want to know George Murphy is interested in you for the next biopic he's directing. His first pick, Kevin Brady, pulled out at the last minute after he'd gotten studio approval. He's in a real pickle to cast in the next few months and you're on the short list. Since you've always wanted to work with him, I was under the impression you might want to talk strategy on how to bring your name to the top of the list. But since you have other priorities, I'm going to fight for other clients who want it bad enough."

Dane wanted to strangle Jason. He didn't appreciate his tone, but he'd been right to call him. George was *the* director he wanted to work with. Dane never thought he'd get a chance to read for him because he'd been seen as the pretty boy for years. But his latest film had shown all the doubters that he had some acting chops. However, he and Jason both needed a time-out to let cooler heads prevail. "I'll call you later." Dane swung open Jason's door and stormed out.

Once he was in the car, Dane wondered if he was a fool for considering making such a leap. He and Iris had known each other for only several months, but it felt as if he'd known her a lifetime. Iris wasn't like other women who saw only his face and physique, or were only after him for his money and fame. Dane was under no illusion that if he didn't have his good looks and the money to back it up they'd ever come near him. None of them wanted to get to know *him*. It was why he didn't allow people to get too close. Jason was right about that. He didn't trust easily.

But Iris was special. She wasn't just a selfless mother. She was a good listener, a caring daughter and… Well, when it came to the bedroom, they were very compatible. He loved her responsiveness. To his touch. To his kisses. He loved her little moans when he was deep inside her. After Jayden's party, he'd almost said he loved her but thankfully caught himself in time. It was cliché to say those three little words while in the throes of passion. When he said them aloud, Dane wanted them to be real and meaningful.

The question was whether she would say yes to his proposal. And there was only one way to find out: he'd have to ask.

"So you and Dane are officially a thing," Shelly said to Iris later that afternoon. Her sister had come to Jayden's chemo appointment to show her solidarity. "Who would have ever thought it?"

Iris shrugged. "I'm just as surprised as you are." When he'd asked her to attend the movie premiere a few days ago, she'd been on cloud nine. It had been exciting and scary being part of Dane's world. The lights, the cameras, the questions shouted at him. Women had begged for his autograph and worn T-shirts printed with Dane's face. He was a superstar, but he was *with* her. It had seemed surreal that at the end of the night, she got to go home with him.

"When I met Dane that day in the hospital, my mind was on Jayden and finding a donor. I—I never thought my search would end up with me not only finding his match, but his father too."

"And someone for you?" Shelly finished. "Admit it, Iris. You've fallen for Dane."

Iris hadn't chosen to fall in love with Dane. She'd thought it was a crush because he was good-looking and famous, but if she was honest with herself, she had to admit she loved him. "Yes, I have."

Shelly beamed with pleasure. "I'm so happy for you, Iris. You deserve it and so much more."

"Dane and I haven't really talked about where this is all going. I mean, we've talked about Jayden and his future, but never ours. We've been so focused on Jayden. He caught a cold, I don't know from where. I've been so careful. Anyway, Dr. Lee is pushing back the transplant date. She wants to be sure he's healthy enough to receive the stem cells.

"Sis, I'm sorry to hear that. You must be outta your mind with worry."

"I am. Worrying about Jayden and now this thing with Dane—I have no idea what he wants."

"Don't you think it's time you asked?"

"I don't want to smother him or seem needy."

"I understand, but you also have to tell him how you feel and what *you* want," Shelly admonished.

"What if he doesn't want the same thing?"

"Then you'll co-parent Jayden and get him through this crisis."

"You make it sound so easy," Iris responded, when she knew it was far from that. There were so many variables.

"Love never is," Shelly said. "I only hope to find the kind of love you've found with Dane one day."

Iris smiled and hoped the fairy-tale ending her sister was envisioning would really come true.

Once Jayden was settled in at home after his treatment, her doorbell rang. It was one of Dane's security guards. "Ms. Iris, I have Jason Underwood here to see you."

"Yes, I know Jason." Iris nodded in Jason's direction. "But I'm afraid Dane isn't here."

"Yes, I know," Jason responded. "I'm here to speak with you if you have a few minutes."

"Jayden and I were about to eat dinner, but I suppose I can spare some time. Come in." She motioned him inside. "Can I get you anything? Water, tea, coffee?"

Jason shook his head. "Nothing for me. I won't be staying long."

Iris's ears perked at the comment. Yet, he'd come all this way to speak with her. "All right. Please have a seat." She waved him in the direction of her couch and sat in a nearby armchair. "What can I do for you?"

"Well…" He sat down, making a big production out of unbuttoning his jacket to avoid wrinkles, and then looked her directly in the eye. "I was hoping you would let Dane go."

"Pardon?"

"Iris, I know Dane cares a great deal about his son, and you for that matter…"

"But?" Because she suspected that word was the next on this man's tongue. Why else would he have come to her home unannounced and without Dane? Was there something he didn't want Dane to know?

"Your relationship has caused Dane to lose focus. He's tanking his career and blowing off projects when he's at his prime."

Iris swallowed the lump in her throat. "And you think that's my fault? I have no power over Dane."

Jason stared at her incredulously. "C'mon, Iris, you and I both know that's not true. You have his heart." He pointed toward the bedroom. "In there. His son. A son Dane never knew anything about or asked for, quite frankly. For years, he's been focused on becoming an award-winning actor, maybe even directing. But since he's discovered Jayden's existence, Dane hasn't committed to his next project and barely picked up a script."

Iris released a long sigh. "And what would you have me do, Mr. Underwood?"

"Let him go. He didn't ask to be a father. Never wanted to be one from what he told me," Jason responded. "Yet he has a ready-made family in you and Jayden."

"And we're the albatross around his neck, dragging him under?" Iris finished for him. When Jason looked down at his designer loafers, she knew that was what he'd meant. "You don't think I'm good enough for him, do you?"

Jason shook his head. "It has nothing to do with that."

"Bull crap!" Iris jumped to her feet. "I know I'm not some Hollywood starlet who can keep Dane's name in the papers, but I care. Probably more than anyone ever has."

"Then if you do, you'll do what's best for him," Jason responded smoothly, rising to his feet and buttoning his suit jacket. "And let him do what he does best—get in front of the camera and act."

She folded her arms across her chest. "I think you should go, Jason."

"I realize what I'm asking you to do isn't easy, Iris." Jason stood and walked toward her, but she stepped backward. Since their first meeting, Iris had gotten the distinct impression Jason didn't much care for her or want her in Dane's life. "But if you do what's right, I'll ensure Dane always provides for Jayden. You will want for nothing."

"Because everything comes down to money for you, doesn't it?" Iris countered. "Well, it's not the be-all and end-all for me, *Jason*. I don't want Dane for his money. I never have. All I've ever wanted is for that little boy—" she motioned toward the bedroom "—to be happy and healthy. Meeting Dane was…" Her voice trailed off and she walked to the front door and held it open.

Jason peered at her for several seconds. "You love him. I can see that. And if you do, you'll let him go." And with that statement, he gave her one final glare before leaving.

Iris slammed the door after him. How dare he come into her home and tell her what to do. He had no right! He was one of the many people who wanted something from Dane while she—she just wanted to love him. But was it enough? Would it ever be enough?

On some level, despite his protests to the contrary, Dane loved the glitz, the glamour and the fame. Why else would he continue to do what he did year in and year out? Yet she was certain he'd found an inner peace when he was with her and Jayden. Or was she fooling herself because she was so in love with him?

Perhaps she was a fool for believing they were building something strong and enduring. Maybe Dane had sent Jason here because he was too afraid to tell her that all *this* was too much. A new son who needed a bone marrow donor. A new lover with her hang-ups. His future would be golden if he didn't have her and Jayden bringing him down. And she would never want to get in the way of Dane reaching for the stars. Because when you loved someone, you were willing to sacrifice for them.

And she loved Dane. But was she prepared to show him how much? Was she strong enough to let Dane go so he could soar?

Dane used the key Iris gave him to enter her small bungalow later that evening. He hated that he could no longer stop by without being accosted by the press. Several of the paparazzi had taken to camping out at Iris's home in the hopes they'd catch him stopping by. Social media was always abuzz with his comings and goings and how often he visited his son, but he wasn't going to let that stop him.

He wanted to see Iris. Hear her teasing laugh and, if Jayden had been put to bed, turn it into a quivering sigh. Sex with Iris was intensely gratifying and by far the best of his life. And when they were together, he wanted to stay with her forever and damn if that didn't amaze him.

She greeted him at the door, brushing her soft lips across his and sliding her arms up his back. Dane's chest tightened and his lips sought hers in a purely carnal kiss. A sultry moan escaped Iris's lips. He lost his head completely and swept his hands over her. Desire stabbed hard through him and he hauled her closer, cupping her behind until she was up against his body and the clear evidence of his need pressed between them.

He drew his head back a fraction. His breathing was ragged and choppy, but he managed to speak. "Hello."

She laughed. "Hello to you too."

His eyes darted around the room, but the lights were muted. He could tell she'd been reading in the armchair because a book was lying face down next to a glass of red wine. "Where's Jayden?"

"Already in bed. Chemo drained him and he couldn't wait up for you. I'm sorry."

"Don't be. I got delayed with some errands and meant to be here sooner," Dane said. "So it's just us?"

She grinned. "Yes."

"Why don't we head to the bedroom?" Dane suggested. He was eager to get Iris naked so he could do all sorts of wicked things to her.

Iris's room was a third of the size of his master suite in the Hollywood Hills, but Dane didn't care. He didn't care that her bed was a queen size compared to his California king that could sleep several people. The cozy room was all Iris. It even smelled like roses and sunshine, because that was how he thought of her.

"Come here, you." She pulled him toward her and reached for his belt. He bent and kissed her again, meshing his lips with hers and slowly sweeping his tongue inside her luscious mouth. She quickly helped him out of his clothes while he took his time stripping her bare. He touched every part of her with soft, tender kisses. She trembled, arching against him. In her eyes, he saw the need he'd felt all day. He used his fingers and mouth to tease, tempt and stretch, keeping her pleasure just out of reach.

Iris fought back. Her mouth went to his throat and her lips danced a wild tango on his neck. It made him feel raw and exposed. "Iris…"

She smiled and rolled atop him. Having her skin on his inflamed him and he murmured words of encouragement as she took him in her hand and lined him up against her wet opening. Her searing gaze burned into his as she sank onto him. Then she rocked her hips, undulating against him, taking him deeper and deeper until she had him to the hilt. It was searing, slow and sublime. They were so close, nothing could come between them. If this wasn't love, Dane wasn't sure what was.

A wave of emotion clogged his throat and Dane knew he wanted to be with Iris forever. He looked into her eyes and gripped her hips tightly as he bucked underneath. "Yes, Iris. *Yes. Give me all of you.*" He rammed upward and Iris clung to him, riding him as they both hurtled straight to the stratosphere.

Afterward she fell forward on top of him, and he wrapped his arms around her. She'd never been more beautiful to him than she was at this moment, glowing from his lovemaking. He whispered the words he could no longer keep contained. "I love you, Iris."

But when he glanced down, Iris was sound asleep on his chest. He grinned. There would be plenty of other times to tell her he'd fallen madly and deeply in love with her.

Fifteen

Iris was up early the next morning. She was already showered and dressed when Dane wandered into the kitchen bare-chested and wearing pajama bottoms. He looked sleepy eyed and sexy as hell. Last night after they'd made love, he'd told her he loved her. *And she'd heard him.* But she'd feigned sleep because she'd been so overwhelmed. She hadn't been the only one feeling this way. Dane loved her too!

But Jason had got in her head yesterday by telling her Dane was throwing away his career and his future if he stayed with her and Jayden. Iris didn't need Jason to point out that she wasn't beautiful like the models and actresses Dane usually dated. She saw it herself every day she looked in the mirror and saw the disfigured flesh from the accident. If they stayed together,

Dane might regret being with her, he might wish he'd held out for someone more beautiful and without all her hang-ups. He deserved better than her, but Iris had finally found happiness. Was it so wrong to want to hang on tight to it? It's why she had told him she loved him back.

If she stayed with Dane, it would hurt him, but if she didn't, he'd be hurt just as much. Would he think she'd been using him for Jayden or for healing herself in some way? Because she had.

For years, Iris had been afraid to put herself out there. She'd been content to live in the shadows and raise her son, never knowing the depth of emotion she could feel for another human being until Dane came along. He was everything she'd been waiting her whole life to find.

And she had to let him go.

Sometime around dawn, Iris realized she was holding Dane back. He was America's Sexiest Man Alive, but he was also a damn fine actor who was destined for greatness. He needed someone who could be in the limelight with him.

Plus, if he stayed with her, his focus wouldn't be on his craft, but on her and Jayden. Jason had been right. Jayden had come down with a cold a few days ago and they'd had to push back the transplant for a couple of weeks until he was fully recovered. Dane had been by her side for days. And she loved him for that. Truly she did. Dane had taken to fatherhood much more easily than anyone thought he would.

Everyone had expected he'd be one of those see-you-on-the-weekend kind of dads. Not Dane. He was invested. And not just because he was giving his bone marrow. He came to all Jayden's treatments. He picked up Jayden from school even if that meant his entire entourage, press included, followed him. Dane was determined to be a better father than his own had been, and he was. That was what made what she *had* to do so hard.

"Good morning." Dane brushed a kiss across her forehead as he moved toward the coffeepot and poured himself a cup. She didn't have a fancy Keurig, just an old-school coffeepot she preprogrammed each evening so she could take a very large YETI mug with her on the way to work.

"Good morning." She avoided his gaze as she set about pulling out cereal and a bowl for Jayden's breakfast. She wasn't sure he was going to eat it. He hadn't had much of an appetite these days due to the chemo treatments.

"You're up early," Dane commented as he sipped his coffee. "Didn't I sufficiently wear you out last night?"

"I have to get to work," Iris said.

"Doesn't your job understand you have a sick child who might require more of you and give you a bit of leeway?"

"It's not needed. Jayden is in the shower and I'm already dressed to get him to chemo," Iris replied tightly. She'd ensured they were on track because she didn't dare spend any more time alone with Dane than was absolutely necessary. Otherwise, she wouldn't have the guts to do what needed to be done. "Some of us can't play around all day. We have to actually make a living."

Dane's dark brown eyes stared at her, clearly disturbed by her tone. "Wow, okay." He scrubbed his jaw. "I guess someone woke up on the wrong side of the bed this morning. I didn't realize it was take-a-shot-at-Dane time."

Iris shrugged. She hated doing this but she saw no other way. "I'm just saying. I have to make a living."

"I could easily take care of you and Jayden. You'd never have to worry about anything but staying by Jayden's side and being there for him when he needs you."

Damn him. He was going to make it harder for her to walk away. "As kind and generous as that is, I don't take handouts, Dane."

"It wouldn't be a handout!" he spat, slamming his coffee cup onto the kitchen table and splashing it all over.

"I'll clean it up." Iris went for a dishrag, but Dane grabbed her forearm.

"Jayden is my son too and I'd like to do my part in taking care of him and supporting you."

"You're doing your part by donating your bone marrow," Iris stated. "But as for me? I've got this and so does my family. We've been doing it for nearly seven years before we knew about you. Please just go back to your life. I'm sure there's plenty of things you should be doing other than getting mired in the muck of our lives."

Dane frowned. "What the hell, Iris? Where is this

coming from? We had an incredible night last night and…and this morning you're acting cold and distant. What's going on?"

"Don't you get it, Dane? I'm letting you go. I'm giving you a free pass to go back to your life and do whatever it was you were doing before you met me."

Hurt was etched across his face, and Iris hated that she was the one putting it there.

"What if I don't want a free pass?"

"That's too bad because I'm giving it to you," Iris responded. "It's over, Dane. You and me. I won't stand in the way of you having a relationship with your son. I wouldn't do that, but…" Her voice trailed off.

"It's not easy giving someone the brush-off, is it?" Dane asked. "Trust me, I know. I've done it. And you know why, Iris? Because you don't want to do this. I have no idea what's got into you, but perhaps it's best if I leave."

He started for the door, but Iris said, "I would like my key back."

Dane spun around to face her, and Iris nearly lost it. His deep brown eyes were filled with despair. She was breaking his heart as well as her own. It was a risk, letting Dane go, but if he was the man she knew him to be, he wouldn't abandon Jayden. He'd still donate his bone marrow and be a father to Jayden. He just wouldn't be with Iris. But in the long run, she was doing what was best for both of them. They were from two different worlds and he needed to be free to pursue his passion.

"I knew you had issues, Iris, but I thought we'd addressed them. I thought you trusted me, but clearly I was wrong. They go much deeper than even I imagined."

"Don't you dare bring my scars into this." She pointed at him. "You don't get to put this on me like I'm the one with the problem!"

"Aren't you?" Dane asked. "You're the one who out of nowhere is turning tail and running as fast as you can from a good thing. Am I getting too close, Iris? Is that the problem? Is being in the light with me too much?"

"Oh, that's rich coming from you. You *have* to live in the limelight. You feed off all the adoration of your fans. I saw you the other night when we went to the premiere. You were eating it up with a spoon."

"It's my job!" Dane responded hotly. "All those people stood in line for hours for a glimpse or picture of me and, God forbid, an autograph. So yeah, I played my part, but it doesn't mean I'm a narcissist."

She knew he wasn't self-absorbed, but she had to push him away. "No, Dane, you're just doing the right thing like you always do."

"What the hell does that mean?"

"C'mon, let's be honest here. The only reason you're with me is because I'm Jayden's mother. And I get it, okay? You want to make sure our son has a better home life than you did growing up, but I'm releasing you of your obligation."

"That's a low blow, Iris. My family has nothing to do with why I'm with you."

Iris shrugged. "Does it matter now anyway? I've said my piece, Dane, and now it's time for you to leave."

"Just like that?" he asked incredulously.

When she didn't answer, he merely turned and left her standing in the kitchen staring after him. Several minutes later, he returned and she was still standing in the exact same place. He didn't look at her. He merely placed her front door key on the table between them, then he strode out of the room. She heard the door slam moments after.

Iris grabbed the top of the nearest chair and crumpled into it. Tears stabbed at her eyes and she tried to blink them back, but she couldn't. She let them fall.

A door opened and Iris heard the pitter-patter of feet and looked up to see Jayden. "Did I hear the front door? Where's Daddy?" He glanced around and then behind him.

Iris wiped the tears away. "He had to leave a bit early, but I'm sure you'll see him soon." But she wouldn't. Iris doubted she'd ever see him again.

Dane shook his head in disbelief as his driver drove him to his Venice Beach house. He still couldn't believe it. Why was she turning her back on him? On the family they'd been creating?

All his life, he'd desperately wanted to feel like he was a part of the Stewart family, but he'd always felt he was an outsider among his own kin. Fallon and their father had always had a special relationship and as for Nora, theirs wasn't the typical mother-son connection. He and his mother couldn't be more different.

It was why he'd left Austin to come to Los Angeles. It was here he discovered he belonged in front of a camera. He could come alive and become somebody else. Was it because he'd never truly liked who he was to begin with?

With Iris and Jayden, Dane felt like he finally belonged. He had a family to call his own. He hadn't even realized he'd needed that until the thought of not being part of one left him cold and empty inside. Since he'd found he had a son, Dane hadn't felt trapped. Instead, a scared yet wondrous joy had taken root inside him and he'd felt happy. Happier than he'd been in a long time. Of course he was angry life had dealt Jayden a raw deal with his disease, but Dane felt strongly the bone marrow transplant would work and if it didn't, they'd try everything until his boy was healed.

And then there was Iris. Beautiful, sweet Iris. It had been only several months, but in their short time together, he'd felt comfort and ease, as well as laughter and sorrow—not to mention desire and passion. When he was with her, he lost total control and rather than scaring him, he'd given in to it. He'd allowed himself to feel whatever he was feeling because Iris wasn't like any woman he'd ever met. She wasn't trying to *get* anything from him and because of that, his feelings had grown.

At first, he hadn't been able to identify them because other than Fallon he'd never really loved anyone, but Iris was easy to love. And now that he'd finally found *the one*, he was afraid of losing her. But what could he do? She'd all but kicked him out of her home.

Eventually the SUV came to a halt and Dane hopped out and punched in the code. His bodyguards knew better than to come in. He was in a surly mood and he needed to be alone to lick his wounds in private. Once inside, he slammed the door and immediately began stripping off his clothes. A punishing swim in the ocean was exactly what he needed to take the edge off.

An hour later Dane felt no better, even after letting the waves wash over him. He was angry. Angry with Iris for turning her back on him. Even though he'd never thought about having a family, he'd thought they were going in that direction. Instead, he felt as if he'd been sucker punched by the woman he loved.

After showering and dressing, Dane reached for his phone and used FaceTime to call the one person he could turn to.

"Hey, Dane." Fallon's image appeared on the screen. "To what do I owe the pleasure of a call at this time, and on a weekday, no less?"

"Iris dumped me and I have no idea why."

"What?" The stunned expression on Fallon's face must have been exactly how Dane looked when Iris delivered her harsh words this morning. "Dane, what are you talking about?"

"This morning, after we'd had such a wonderful night together, Iris started a fight. Told me she didn't have time to spend cuddling with me. Pretty much acted as if I was insignificant in her or Jayden's life. I don't understand any of it, Fallon. Why would she do something like this?"

"This makes absolutely no sense. The Iris I met

clearly adores you. She was so excited to surprise you with our visit. It showed me how invested she was in your relationship. I can't believe she'd cast you aside so easily."

"Well, she did," Dane stated, running his hand over his head. "And for the life of me I don't know why. I've tried to be the best father I can for Jayden."

"And you have been, Dane. I mean, you never expected to become a father after being a sperm donor, but I've seen you rise to the occasion. No pun intended."

"Thanks, Fallon."

"No, I mean it. When I was there I saw how much you loved your son and that you'd do anything for him. And for Iris."

"Then why did she push me away as if I was nothing to her? Do you have any idea how humiliating and embarrassing this is? I've risked everything to be with her, Fallon. My reputation, my career, my *brand*, because I thought we were building a future together. And now I find it's made of sand."

"Don't say that, Dane. Don't give up on her. There has to be an explanation for Iris's actions."

"If you can find one, I'm listening. Because all I hear right now is my team telling me to take it slow. 'You don't have to have a ready-made family, Dane. You can be a father to your son without being Iris's husband.' But no, I had to go all in, guns blazing."

"Wait a sec." Fallon was silent for several minutes. "Did you say *husband*?"

Dane rolled his eyes. He'd been hoping to gloss over

that part, but Fallon had heard him. "Yeah, I was seriously considering asking Iris to marry me."

"Marry you? Omigod, Dane, that's wonderful!"

"Like hell it is," Dane roared. "She wants no part of me, Fallon, and I'm not going to sit at home spinning my wheels trying to figure her out. I'm going to take charge of my life and do what I do best—make movies."

"Oh, Dane, running away won't solve the problem."

"Really, Fallon? As I recall, you kept Gage at arm's length for months when you were pregnant with Dylan."

"Hey…that's not fair. And that situation was different. Gage lied to me and violated my trust. We had a lot to work through. You and Iris can overcome your issues if you just give it a chance."

"No," Dane said definitively. "I'll be there for Jayden, but me and Iris are done."

Dane ended the call with his sister minutes later, but he didn't feel any better. The thought of starting another movie left him cold, but what choice did he have? Iris didn't want him. He could go back to the life he had before, when he had an endless selection of willing bedmates. But the thought of sleeping with anyone else made his skin crawl and he couldn't stomach thinking of Iris with another man.

All he wanted to do right now was call her and make sure she was okay. He was a fool. She'd probably felt only gratitude to him for reintroducing her to sex. He should be flattered and move on, but he couldn't. And once it was time for the bone marrow transplant, he would have to see Iris more frequently. How was he supposed to navigate being beside her but not with her? There was an ache in his chest that wouldn't go away and he was beginning to realize what it was.

He was heartbroken.

Sixteen

"I want you to arrange a meeting with George Murphy," Dane told Jason when his manager stopped by the following day.

"What brought on the change?" Jason inquired. "I thought you were going to focus on 'your family.'" He made air quotes with his hands.

"If you're talking about my son, I'll be there when I can for his treatments and certainly back in enough time for the transplant."

"Actually no, I wasn't talking about Jayden. Correct me if I'm wrong, but weren't you going to ask Iris to marry you?"

"Iris and I are over," Dane said, turning away to face the massive infinity pool in his backyard. He didn't see the look of pure joy cross Jason's face.

"Oh? When did that happen?"

"Does it matter?" Dane asked, turning back around. "All you need to know is I'm taking your advice and focusing on my career."

"I'm ecstatic you're heeding my advice, but are you okay?"

"I will be once I get back to work, so find me something. Anything at this point, but I need to get the bloody hell out of Los Angeles."

"I'm on it," Jason said and then walked toward him to place his hand on his shoulder. "For what it's worth, I'm sorry this happened. I know how much you cared for Iris."

Dane was thankful when Jason had finally gone. He couldn't bear to see the smug look on his face that he was right about Iris and him. How could he have been so wrong?

"Dane, I don't mean to interfere, but are you sure you don't want to take some time, ya know…?" He heard Morgan's voice trail off behind him.

"To mope around and feel sorry for myself that my girl dumped me?" Dane inquired. "No thanks, Morgan. It's better if I get back to work as soon as possible."

"What about your family? Maybe talking to your dad might help. Henry Stewart, right?"

Dane frowned. "Yeah, that's him, but I don't have those kind of parents. Thank you for caring, though."

"You're welcome."

He appreciated his assistant trying to help, but the more he thought about Iris's behavior, the angrier he got. He wanted to go over there and give her a piece of his mind, but in the end it would solve nothing. He'd still be back where he was in this purgatory where his mind and heart were at war. His mind told him to move on, focus on his career, while his heart…his heart told him to fight for what he wanted and never let go.

His mind won out.

It had been seven days, four hours, thirty-eight minutes and five seconds since Dane had walked out her door. Iris recalled to the minute detail the look of utter hurt that crossed his beautiful face when she'd told him to leave his key and get out.

She'd done it for all the right reasons. Because she *loved* him and would do anything for him, including give him up for the greater good. Dane was tanking his career to be with her and Jayden and she couldn't let that happen.

But why did it have to hurt so hard?

She missed sleeping beside him night after night, missed cuddling close to the rock-hard wall of his chest. She craved the intimacy they shared. She missed rousing him from sleep with a kiss on his sensuous mouth and the intoxicatingly addictive passion Dane brought out in her. Somehow he'd seen through her—to the loneliness she'd carried with her for years.

Another part of her was angry too.

Why hadn't Dane fought harder to save what they had? Iris knew it was irrational to think this way when she was the cause of the breakup. Somewhere deep down, Iris wanted Dane to fight for her, fight for them. Show her he wouldn't give up on her so easily when times were tough. But he hadn't. He'd accepted the easy way out and left, leaving her shell-shocked.

The pain was so excruciating, Iris hadn't wanted to get out of bed. If it hadn't been for Jayden coming to wake her up, he would have been late for his chemo treatments. Jayden was starting to suspect something was wrong because he'd never seen her in the dumps. The only time Iris had been like this was after the accident. She hadn't wanted to leave the house then because she'd felt ugly. It wasn't healthy for her to stay in this headspace and Iris knew it was pointless to wallow in the grief, but she couldn't seem to help herself.

So it was no surprise on the eighth day when her sister made an appearance. "Iris?" Shelly called out as she let herself inside the bungalow. "Where are you?"

"In here," Iris called out from her bedroom.

Minutes later, Shelly appeared in the doorway. She was dressed for work in a knee-length skirt, silk blouse and pumps. "Why are you still in bed? It's the middle of the week, for Christ's sake."

"I'm tired," Iris said, sinking lower into the covers.

"That's not what my nephew tells me." Shelly came into the room and opened all the blinds before sitting on the bed.

How was it that, in just a short time, Iris had come to think of the right side as *her* side of the bed? Why? Because Dane favored the left side, that was why. "Did Jayden rat on me?"

"If you mean did he call his auntie to tell me his mother won't get out of bed and has missed the last week of work? Then yes, he ratted you out."

Iris leaned backward against the pillows. "I'm sorry he did that. I'm fine."

"No, you're not fine." Shelly pulled back the covers so she could see Iris's face.

Iris shuddered to think what she must look like. After crying on and off for days, her eyes were probably swollen and puffy, her nose red from constantly blowing it. "Go home, Shelly, and leave me be."

"I can't do that, Iris. Jayden needs you to be on top of your game, especially if his father is MIA these days. And two, whatever it is, whatever is going on between you and Dane, surely it can be fixed."

Iris shook her head. "Don't you get it, Shelly? It can't be fixed!" she wailed. "Don't you think if it could, I wouldn't be in this state?"

Shelly clutched her chest. "What on earth could have happened? Last time I saw Dane was at our parents' for dinner a couple of weeks ago, and the man was walking on cloud nine."

"We broke up," Iris blurted. "Correction. I broke up with Dane."

Shelly's eyes grew large. "Why would you do such a thing?"

"Because— Look at me, Shelly. I'm nothing special. I'm not like the beautiful starlets with the perfect bodies he's used to being with."

"You're not giving yourself enough credit. You're more than just your looks."

"But I'm bringing Dane down. He's worked so hard to get to where he is and he's turning down movies because of me."

"And Jayden," Shelly clarified. "Let's not forget he has a son."

"A son he had no idea he had. And now all of a sudden, we've blown through his life like a tornado, leaving nothing but damage in our wake."

"That's not true, Iris. I *saw* how happy Dane was. How happy you were. *Together.* I'm not wrong about that. You told me yourself you were in love with him. Why would you break up with him?"

"To set him free. I don't want him to feel obligated to be with me."

"So he could be America's Sexiest Man Alive? Did you for once think that maybe, just maybe, Dane might want more in his life than the superficiality of Hollywood? That having you and Jayden in his life has grounded him?"

Tears slid down Iris's cheeks. "If—if I allowed myself to think that, Shelly, then I've just made the biggest mistake of my life."

"I'm sorry to tell you, sis, but you did," Shelly stated matter-of-factly. "You're not holding Dane back. You've given him so much more. A son, love and a family. Sure that's worth fighting for. So my question to you is, what are you going to do to fix it?"

"I can't fix it."

"Au contraire," Shelly said. "I know how stubborn you can be when you put your mind to something. Remember how adamant you were about no more reconstructive surgeries? Because I do. Be that determined again. Show Dane that woman. Tell him you love him and I promise you he'll take you back."

Was Shelly right? Should she try to repair the damage she'd made of their relationship? As for Jayden, she was certain Dane would still donate because he'd been willing to do so before he knew he was Jayden's father. However, their relationship would be strained and she didn't want to do anything that would jeopardize Jayden's well-being. Not to mention he'd miss having his father in his life day-to-day. She had to do whatever she could to repair the rift she'd caused between her and Dane. Because they deserved love and happiness for themselves and their son.

"What if it's too late? What if he turns me away?" Iris was scared that she might have done irreparable harm.

Shelly smiled. "You showing up to fight for him should be more than enough to melt the ice. But you'll have to take a risk and lay yourself bare and be completely honest with him."

Iris threw back her covers and stood. "All right, you've talked some sense into me. I'm going to get my man back."

"'Atta girl!" Shelly cheered.

Iris just hoped Dane would forgive her and if he didn't, she'd keep trying until he did.

"Can't you get anything right? I asked for a Perrier," Dane snapped at Morgan the following day.

"Of course. I'll get right on that," Morgan said before rushing away.

Dane leaned back in the director's chair and sighed. He should never have agreed to this movie. It was like the romantic comedies he'd done early in his career when he was trying to make a name for himself. The last couple of years, he'd been more selective about the projects he chose. He wanted them to have range for him to showcase his acting muscles. Instead, he'd taken what he could get to keep his mind off Iris, and was faced with memorizing bland clichéd dialogue. It was driving him crazy.

He hadn't meant to snap at Morgan. It wasn't her fault he was in a bad mood. He'd been this way since he'd left Iris's home that fateful morning over a week ago.

Staying in Los Angeles hadn't been an option. There were too many reminders of the places they'd gone or things they'd done. Even his beach house wasn't an oasis anymore because all he could think about was the first time he'd made love to Iris. How beautiful and intense it had been.

Dane doubted he could ever go back there now. It was too painful. So when Jason told him this movie was teed up and ready to go in Kitty Hawk, North Carolina, he'd jumped on the opportunity to get out of town. He'd regretted it almost immediately. Despite the scenic beachside location, he was miserable. His heart wasn't in the role; he wanted meatier, grittier material. But most of all he wanted his life back. He wanted the life he'd created with Iris and Jayden.

His cell phone vibrated and Dane answered. "Hey, sis."

"Are you being mean to Morgan?"

Was he being filmed on *Candid Camera* or something? Dane jumped up from his chair and glanced around. That's when he saw a honey blonde walking toward him on the sand.

"Fallon? What are you doing here?" Dane asked, ending their call.

"Saving you from yourself, it would seem," she stated with one hand on her hip. She was wearing a maxi dress and holding a pair of strappy sandals. "When I called your house to check on you, I was informed by your maid you'd left to work on a film in North Carolina. After you called me last week, I'd already planned to come to you. I just needed to get childcare arranged. But then Morgan called me and told me you'd been a tyrant all week and thought you might need your big sis to give you a kick in the rear, so here I am."

Dane grinned. "Morgan called you?"

"She cares about you. She's been your assistant for over a year now. And she gives a crap about you despite how you treat her."

"Yeah, she's a good kid."

"She's twenty-four years old."

Dane chuckled. "I don't know what it is, but now that I'm a father, I feel older. Wiser somehow."

"Wiser?" Fallon raised a brow. "I don't know about that." She looped her arm through his. "Walk with me for a bit."

"All right." They walked in silence for several minutes before he said, "I'm surprised Gage let you out of his sight."

"Gage has mellowed, Dane. I admit when we were

first together he was rather dark and intense. But he's grown. We both have. And I can see you have too."

Dane's brow furrowed. "You can?"

"Oh, yes. I may have joked with you back there, but you've matured greatly, Dane. You no longer think about just yourself. You put others' needs ahead of your own."

"Well, being a parent kind of forces you to do that."

She nodded. "It does. But that's only part of your growth. You've grown because you've finally opened yourself up to love."

Dane shook his head. "No, you're wrong. I might have fancied myself in love, but it was one-sided. Iris doesn't love me."

"I don't believe that. And neither do you. Otherwise you wouldn't be so angry and biting everyone's heads off. Besides, I know a woman in love and Iris has been bitten by the love bug."

"What would you have me do, Fallon? She sent me away."

"Fight, Dane. Fight for what you want. Don't let anyone, anything or any career—" she motioned around them to the set "—get in your way. I took a private jet here and it's waiting to take you home and back to Iris."

"What if she sends me away again?" Dane inquired.

"Maybe she ran scared," Fallon suggested. "But if you coming back doesn't show her that you're absolutely made for each other, nothing else will."

Dane pulled Fallon into his arms and gave her a squeeze. "Thank you, sis."

He was going to extricate himself from this movie

and get back to Los Angeles. This time he would tell Iris how he felt. He would tell her and show her exactly how much he loved her and their life together. And this time, he wasn't taking no for an answer.

Seventeen

Iris was nervous as she drove to Dane's set in the Outer Banks of North Carolina that afternoon. She'd never been to the state before, much less to the East Coast, so she was way out of her comfort zone. But she had to do this.

On the nearly seven-hour flight from Los Angeles to Norfolk, Virginia, Iris had had plenty of time to think. Shelly was right; she'd made a big mistake listening to Jason and giving in to her fears about whether she and Dane truly had a shot. How would she ever know, if she gave up on them at the first sign of adversity? She was guilty of the very same thing she was accusing him of.

Dane had been shocked when she'd told him they were over. He'd told her he loved her, for Christ's sake! And if there was a chance, any chance they could be happy together, have a family, then she had to be willing to risk it all, including her own embarrassment at coming to Dane's movie shoot. She owed him and herself that much.

Iris was thankful when she phoned Morgan that Dane's assistant hadn't hung up on her. In fact, she seemed ecstatic to hear from Iris. She'd shared that Dane had been miserable since he'd left her over a week ago and was ripping everyone to shreds. No one was off-limits. Iris knew Dane wasn't that person, but he was hurting and she was the reason. She apologized profusely to Morgan and hoped her coming would change things. Morgan understood and gave her all the details on where to find them, and said there'd be a set pass waiting for her.

When she arrived, Morgan immediately came to meet her. "I'm so glad you're here," she said. "I think *you* are exactly what, or shall I say *who* Dane needs to see."

"Do you really think so?" Iris asked. "He's probably really upset with me."

"And he may not be happy with my interference either," Morgan said with a snort, "but I had to do something. You guys are so cute together." She looped a lanyard over Iris's head. "He's down that way." She pointed toward the set.

"Thanks, Morgan." Iris gave her a nervous smile and started walking toward her future.

Dane walked briskly with Fallon through the sand to get back up the embankment to the main road. He needed to get his wheels. He was anxious to get home to Los Angeles as fast as he could.

Dane came to a stop by the stairs leading to the parking lot. "You don't mind traveling to Los Angeles and then back to Austin?"

"Not at all. I'm here to help, but it looks like I don't need to..."

Dane glanced up. Surely his eyes were deceiving him. Iris couldn't be standing at the top of the stairs leading to the beach—here in the Outer Banks of North Carolina? He blinked several times to make sure she was real and that he hadn't imagined her. But when he looked again, she was smiling down at him and his heart swelled.

"Iris?"

She nodded.

"I'm going to go now," Fallon said, backing away from Dane. "I think the two of you—" she used her index and middle finger to point at them "—have a lot to say to each other and don't need an audience."

Dane looked back at his sister and mouthed the words, "Thank you." He watched her for several beats as she walked down the beach until her figure became a speck on the horizon. Then he looked up, only to realize Iris had beat him to the punch. She had descended the stairs and was standing in front of him.

"What—what are you doing here?" He couldn't get the words out. He was tongue-tied.

"I had to see you," Iris replied. "I—I had to tell you I made a mistake and I was fool to let you go."

A lump formed in Dane's throat and he wasn't sure he could speak, so he listened.

"I thought I was doing what was best for you. Jason said that—"

"Jason?" he interrupted her almost immediately. "What does Jason have to do with any of this?"

"He came to see me. He said you were tanking your career by being with me and Jayden, giving up good projects, and it was going to ruin everything you'd worked so hard to build. I couldn't let that happen."

"So you told me to go?"

She nodded and an errant tear fell from one of her eyes. She wiped it away with the back of her hand. "Yes. I said horrible things to you that day. Words I deeply regret. I wish I could take them all back because I didn't mean any of them, Dane. I only said them because I knew if I didn't hurt you, you would stay and I needed you to go so you could be happy."

"Happy?" His voice rose. "Iris, don't you get it? You and Jayden make me happy," Dane responded. "You're my world."

"We are?"

"Of course you are. Haven't I told you from the moment I first met you? It's always been you. I don't want anyone else. Because none of them, none of these actresses or celebrities—" he pointed behind him toward the set "—are *you*. You're the woman I'd measure every other woman against anyway, and they'd be severely lacking."

"You don't have to say that."

"Damn it, Iris. When will you get it? It's you I love.

It's only you." Dane hadn't intended to blurt out his feelings, but seeing Iris so unexpectedly gave him hope. She hadn't traveled cross-country to his movie set just to say hello. She'd come for a reason. He just prayed and hoped she felt the same way about him.

A shadow of a smile crossed her face and it filled him with such joy. He'd been missing *this* for the last week. It had felt like the sunshine had gone from his life and there was nothing but dark storm clouds left.

Her next words were softly spoken, but he heard them all the same. "I love you too, Dane."

Dane released a long sigh because it was a balm to his aching heart. "You do?"

"Yes, I came all this way to tell you. I was a fool for listening to the haters and the doubters who don't believe in us and I'm done with it. If you can forgive me, if you can accept my most heartfelt apology for hurting you and putting us through this week of agony, then I'm yours. Mind, body and soul."

"Oh, Iris." Dane swept the woman he loved into his arms, anchoring her to him while his mouth lowered to kiss hers. Iris's lips immediately opened under his and she accepted his invitation, fusing her mouth with his as they sought to get closer together. Her kiss rocked his soul and promised him a lifetime of happiness.

"We should get out of here," he said. His breathing was ragged and edgy, and he was hungry for her. He couldn't wait to run his hands all over her.

"Please," Iris murmured. "I can't wait to be alone with you too."

Taking her by the hand, Dane led Iris away to start the next phase of their journey.

It wasn't too late. Dane could and would forgive her. Iris had never been so grateful in her entire life, except when Dr. Lee had told her they'd found a donor match. When she'd seen Dane in dark jeans and a navy T-shirt standing at the base of the stairs just now, she'd nearly lost her nerve, but when he'd looked at her and given her one of his signature devastating smiles, she'd seen the truth there. She'd been right to come. He'd wrapped his arms around her, and it was exactly what she wanted—what she needed. She needed him more than words could ever express. And she could see he needed her too.

Hand in hand, Dane led her to an SUV that was his to use for the duration of the movie project. The drive to the vacation rental house on stilts where Dane was staying didn't take long. When they got there, they quickly exited the vehicle and rushed up the stairs, eager to be alone together like two love-crazed teenagers.

They didn't make it to the bedroom. Dane tumbled her back onto the couch. He knelt over her, his hand slipping behind her head so he could loosen her topknot. Her hair was free within seconds and he sat back on his haunches to wrench his T-shirt off. Iris stared up at him and inhaled his delicious, rich, woodsy scent she loved so much.

His gaze caught hers and he smiled wickedly. "I've missed you, Iris."

"And I've missed you."

He began unbuttoning her blouse and before she knew it, both that and her bra were tossed to the floor beside the couch. Then he kissed her long and hard until she was breathless and she didn't care. She wanted to hold his mouth prisoner against hers forever.

Hot, all-consuming desire enveloped them and they fell onto the rug, laughing. But that didn't keep them from their kiss. They greedily feasted on one another. She was holding on to his muscular shoulders while his arms molded to the shape of her. She could feel him all around her and Iris welcomed his dominance because only Dane could make her feel so alive.

Her legs naturally splayed to accommodate him and he obliged, moving from her mouth to her breasts. And when he fastened his mouth on her tightly budded nipple, a flame of excitement shot straight to her belly and she moved her hips instinctively to *feel* him.

"I want to do things slowly," Dane murmured against her bosom. "I want to savor you."

The sweep of his lips against her skin was like a hypnotic swirl against her flesh. Iris no longer thought about her imperfections when she was with Dane. She thought only of him. "There will be time for slow later," Iris replied. "I need you now."

He gave her a devilish grin and lifted off her long enough to peel her jeans and panties from her trembling body, baring her completely to his gaze, to his touch, to his mouth. Then he was stripping his remaining clothes from his body and joining her on the floor.

But before they made love, she had something to

say. Something that needed to be said. She grasped both sides of his cheeks with her palms. "I have to say this, Dane, and get it out while I can."

"Whatever it is, sweetheart—" his eyes peered into hers "—you can tell me."

"I'm sorry," Iris responded. "I'm truly sorry. And I promise I won't hurt you again. I promise to always fight for you and for everything we have built together. I will be strong for you as you've been strong for me and Jayden, and I won't let anyone or anything come between us again." She was his, body and soul, and she would love him to the day she died, with everything she had. "I love you, Dane."

"I love you more than anything in this world, other than Jayden," he responded.

"More than your career?"

"Yes," Dane stated emphatically. "Now let's quit talking and let's start loving." His lips slanted over hers, his tongue plundering inside her mouth while his hands moved lower to part her thighs. She granted him access, enjoying every sensation, especially when one of his skilled fingers slipped into her tight channel.

"Dane…"

"Yes, baby…" He swirled his fingers across her nub, again and again, sinking deeper and deeper inside her. It felt so incredible she began to shake.

"That's right, Iris. Let go." He slipped out and this time inserted two fingers. Her muscles clenched and began tightening around him; she could feel herself about to come.

But Dane didn't let her. Instead, he slid home inside her and she tilted her hips, welcoming his length while locking her legs around his back. Dane filled her so completely. With clarity Iris knew what she'd found with Dane was life changing. When he moved, she followed, matching him until the pressure began to build and he was surging inside her over and over and over again. Ecstasy came swiftly, suspending them momentarily in time as Dane pumped his release and gave a low groan. He collapsed on top of her before withdrawing to lie beside her, and tried to catch his breath.

Dane turned his head to look at her and whispered, "I love you, Iris."

"I feel the same," she said with a smile.

He sat up and leaned on his forearm, becoming serious. "Yeah, but this time I'm telling you I can't imagine my life without you, and I don't want to live like I did this last week in a half existence. I want to live fully and completely with you and Jayden for as long as we have."

"What are you saying, Dane?"

"I guess I'm going about this all wrong," Dane said. He rose from the floor and slipped on his boxers. "Let me do this the right way." He bent down on one knee. "Iris Turner, will you do me the supreme honor of being my wife?"

The words felt good on Dane's lips and he liked the way they tasted.

Iris bolted upright. Her eyes were wide and luminescent, searching his for an indication he was serious.

He was.

"And before you ask me if I'm sure, Iris, I am. I'm not doing this out of duty. I'm asking you because I want to be with you."

He could see her battling herself, as if she wanted to say something. All he wanted Iris to say was yes. "I wasn't about to say no," Iris responded. "I was just thinking I'd like to wait until Jayden's better."

Dane grinned from ear to ear. "Does that mean…"

Iris chuckled. "It means I'm saying yes. A thousand times, yes!" She threw her arms around him, closing the distance between them. "I can't wait to spend the rest of my life with you."

His lips dipped lower and his mouth found hers in a heady kiss that bloomed with love he'd never known he could find. And Dane gave himself up to the feeling because Iris had shown him how good love could be. It didn't have to be distant like his parents'; it could be wondrous, crazy, joyous and everything in between.

"You seem deep in thought," Iris said, looking up at him.

"I was. For so long I wondered if I'd ever fit in or be a part of a family, but I've found my home with you and Jayden."

But there was one pressing piece of business he still had to attend to when he returned to Los Angeles and it couldn't wait.

"Dane, what are you doing here?" Jason asked when Dane stormed into his manager's office bright and early on Monday. "You should be filming."

After Iris had stunned him with her trip to North

Carolina, they'd taken the weekend to get reacquainted in every sense of the word. But now it was time for business.

"Yeah, I should, Jason, but instead I'm here," Dane replied with a satisfied smile. "To fire you."

"Excuse me?" Jason huffed. "W-what the hell are you talking about, Dane?"

Dane narrowed his eyes. "You know exactly what I'm talking about, Jason. I guess you thought a dumb schmuck like me would never find out that you went behind my back to my woman and lied to her. Put doubts in her head about the relationship."

"I didn't say anything that wasn't true," Jason countered. "You were losing your edge after you worked so hard to get here. I was *helping* save your career. That's my job!"

"Well, I don't need your brand of help anymore. You're fired."

"You can't do that. We have a contract," Jason said.

"That I have the right to terminate on ethical grounds. If you recall, there's a morals clause in the contract."

"I was doing what was best for you and I stand behind that," Jason said. "How else do you think you got here, Dane? I've stood behind you, boosted you up, been your advocate when no one would look at you. And now, you're turning your back on me for a woman who couldn't even get laid to have a kid?"

The punch was quick.

Dane had tried to remain calm, but he wouldn't abide anyone talking ill about Iris. "*That woman* is my fiancée, soon to be my wife, and if you ever disrespect her again, you'll live to regret it."

"I'll blackball you," Jason responded.

Dane laughed. "I'd like to see you try. You must forget who the celebrity is here, who has the star power. Because if you come after me, I promise you I won't rest until I ruin you, Underwood."

"Just go, Dane. I hope you're happy with all that domesticity."

"Oh, you can believe it, I will be," Dane replied. After saying his piece, he strolled out, leaving a stunned Jason staring after him.

When he got outside, Iris was waiting for him in his convertible with the top down surrounded by cameras and reporters eager to get a quote and a glimpse of the enormous rock he'd put on her finger just that morning at the jewelry store.

"You ready?" Iris asked, glancing at him from the driver seat.

"I am." Dane slid inside the car and rode off into the sunset with the woman he loved.

Epilogue

Six months later...

Dane nervously waited under the simple arbor draped in white chiffon and laden with fresh white roses. He glanced around at the family and friends gathered on the sunny La Jolla beach for his simple yet elegant wedding to Iris Turner.

Fallon, Gage and Dylan were there in the first row. Seated beside them was his sister-in-law, Maya. She was holding her new baby girl, Elyse, who was sleeping peacefully. Then there were his parents Henry and Nora Stewart. They'd finally visited Jayden when he was in the hospital and now were attempting to get to know their oldest grandchild. Dane didn't expect much, but he appreciated the effort if nothing else for Jayden's benefit. Whitney was there, but Dane frowned when he didn't see Morgan. *Where is she?* She'd been instrumental in ensuring Iris found him six months ago in North Carolina. And she'd been excited to finally meet his parents.

Dane shook off the unease and glanced at his soon-to-be mother-in-law, who was beaming proudly at him. Charles Turner would be walking Iris down the aisle, while Shelly was her maid of honor. Ayden stood beside him as his best man. It was hard to believe Jason, someone he'd considered a friend, had sold him out and wouldn't be in Ayden's place.

But today wasn't a day for looking back.

He was looking ahead.

And as the waves gently lapped the shore, he saw Iris walk down the aisle in a stunning gown fit for a queen.

His queen.

The ceremony was sweet and heartfelt, with each of them saying vows they'd personally written. The words were easy for Dane because he'd never found a woman quite like Iris. He was proud to stand before God and everyone he knew and pledge his undying love and devotion to her. It was all the more special because Jayden, their ring bearer, was standing by. After all the chemo treatments, the transplant had been a success. Dane had recovered easily once his stem cells were harvested, but had worried incessantly over Jayden. Luckily his son accepted the transplant and after spending months in the hospital under quarantine to prevent any infections, Jayden bounced back. He wasn't 100 percent yet, but his health had improved by leaps and bounds, which was why Dane and Iris felt it was finally time to get hitched.

"I now pronounce you husband and wife," the reverend said. "You may kiss your bride." Dane lifted Iris's veil, pulled her into his arms and planted a big one on her mouth. The kiss wasn't meant to elicit passion, but that was what he felt. Because Iris did it for him. She always had and she always would.

And now she was his forever.

They walked down the aisle with Jayden at their side to their happily ever after.

* * * * *

*If you loved
Dane and Iris's story,
you won't want to
miss it when
Dane's assistant, Morgan,
reveals her big secret,
in the next installment
of The Stewart Heirs.*

*Coming soon
from
Yahrah St. John
and
Harlequin Desire!*

WE HOPE YOU ENJOYED THIS BOOK!

HARLEQUIN® *Desire*

Experience sensual stories of juicy drama and intense chemistry cast in the world of the American elite.

Discover six new books every month, available wherever books are sold!

Harlequin.com

AVAILABLE THIS MONTH FROM
Harlequin® Desire

DUTY OR DESIRE
The Westmoreland Legacy • by Brenda Jackson

Becoming guardian of his young niece is tough for Westmoreland neighbor Pete Higgins. But Myra Hollister, the irresistible new nanny with a dangerous past, pushes him to the brink. Will desire for the nanny distract him from duty to his niece?

TEMPTING THE TEXAN
Texas Cattleman's Club: Inheritance • by Maureen Child

When a family tragedy calls rancher Kellan Blackwood home to Royal, Texas, he's reunited with the woman he left behind, Irina Romanov. Can the secrets that drove them apart in the first place bring them back together?

THE RIVAL
Dynasties: Mesa Falls • by Joanne Rock

Media mogul Devon Salazar is suspicious of the seductive new tour guide at Mesa Falls Ranch. Sure enough, Regina Flores wants to take him down after his father destroyed her family. But attraction to her target might take her down first...

RED CARPET REDEMPTION
The Stewart Heirs • by Yahrah St. John

Dane Stewart is a Hollywood heartthrob with a devilish reputation. When a sperm bank mishap reveals he has a secret child with the beautiful but guarded Iris Turner, their intense chemistry surprises them both. Can this made for the movies romance last?

ONE NIGHT TO RISK IT ALL
One Night • by Katherine Garbera

After a night of passion, Inigo Velasquez learns that socialite Marielle Bisset is the woman who ruined his sister's marriage. A staged seduction to avenge his sister might quell his moral outrage... But will it quench his desire for Marielle?

TWIN SCANDALS
The Pearl House • by Fiona Brand

Seeking payback against the man who dumped her, Sophie Messena switches places with her twin on a business trip with billionaire Ben Sabin. When they are stranded by a storm, their attraction surges. But will past scandals threaten their chance at a future?

**LOOK FOR THESE AND OTHER HARLEQUIN® DESIRE BOOKS
WHEREVER BOOKS ARE SOLD, INCLUDING MOST BOOKSTORES,
SUPERMARKETS, DISCOUNT STORES AND DRUGSTORES.**

COMING NEXT MONTH FROM

HARLEQUIN Desire

Available January 7, 2020
